I0594128

The Banker and the Eagle: The End of Democracy

The Banker Trilogy, Volume 2

Martin Lundqvist

Published by Martin Lundqvist, 2020.

This is a work of fiction. Similarities to real people, places, or events are entirely coincidental.

THE BANKER AND THE EAGLE: THE END OF DEMOCRACY

First edition. September 3, 2020.

Copyright © 2020 Martin Lundqvist.

Written by Martin Lundqvist.

Chapter 1: The attack on the FNN Headquarters, 6th June 2028.

CIA director James Winter was sitting in the FNN Headquarters, over-looking Central Park in New York. The sun was shining outside, and James would almost have been humming on a tune if his business here wasn't so important. "Mr Bucker will meet with you shortly. Would you like a cup of coffee while you are waiting?", Geoffrey Bucker's secretary asked James.

James didn't bother answering and he waved her away. James felt annoyed that Geoffrey didn't consider him important enough to put everything else aside when he requested a meeting. This kind of contemptuous behaviour never happened to Pierre Beaumont.

James realised that wealthy plutocrats were more interested in appeasing the world's richest man, Pierre Beaumont, than appeasing him. James got distracted from that thought when his phone rang. It was Melinda.

James stared at his phone and hesitated. Melinda Barnes was James' subordinate at the CIA, and they had a secret fling. Although James felt closer to her than he had ever felt in his life, he also felt terrified at the same time. Melinda was a straight-and-arrow operator and a true patriot. James feared to get close to her as he had received a lot of money from Pierre for concealing the truth about the Hei Bai Virus outbreak that spread in 2021. The outbreak had killed 300,000 people in New York within a matter of days. Many of them had been world leaders, as the outbreak had coincided with a United Nations summit.

Pierre had orchestrated this biological weapons outbreak. He had caused it so that he could become the wealthiest man in the world from shorting the markets before the outbreak.

To make matters worse, James had not only kept his mouth about Pierre's crimes against humanity. James had also covered up the fact that Pierre's alleged cure for the Hei Bai virus, Reversogene, made by Pierre's pharmaceutical company Axil Azteca, caused infertility and serious liver damage. Millions had died worldwide from Pierre's shoddy drug, and many more had ended up sterile.

James picked up the phone:

- Hi Melinda.

Melinda:

- Hi James. I was worried about you. You are not in your office and you haven't picked up your phone all day.

James:

- I am sorry, Mel. I am meeting someone.

Melinda:

- Is this one of your many women that you're meeting?

A part of James wanted to answer 'yes' to this question. His feelings for Melinda was risky and he wanted to keep her away. But James couldn't make himself brush her off, so he replied:

- No, I am meeting someone for work.

Melinda:

- Who?

James:

- I am sorry, but that's above your pay grade.

Melinda remained silent for a few seconds, and James could imagine how annoyed she was. Melinda broke the silence and she hid her irritation:

- I understand. Are you still bowling with me, Jack, and Joanne tonight?

James:

- Yes, I can't wait to meet those cute troublemakers again. Got to go.
See you tonight.

James hung up the phone. How could it have come to this? Why was he about to swap his life of partying and glamorous women, for being a monogamous boring old stepdad? It didn't make sense, but perhaps that was the way of the heart.

'Mr Bucker will receive you now.' The secretary informed James, who got up and walked towards Geoffrey Bucker's extravagant office.

GEOFFREY BUCKER SMILED as James Winter entered his office. The men shook hands and got seated by an antique mahogany table.

Geoffrey:

- I am sorry to keep you waiting. As the CEO of the Factual News Network, I must report on daily occurrences that affect our world. A great responsibility as you can appreciate.

James shook his head and mocked:

- Oh, I have always thought that FNN stood for Fake News Network. I learn something new every day.

Geoffrey:

- Fake or factual, these are just words. What matters is the impact my news has on the world.

James:

- That is true, and that is why I am here. I have heard rumours about your intentions to report that Reversogene caused a lot of deaths and suffering back in 2022. Tell me why?

Geoffrey:

- I haven't decided yet. But our sources are credible, so that scoop would be a good deed for once.

James:

- That's irrelevant. Revealing the truth would destroy President Mitchell Cent's chance of re-election.

Geoffrey:

- That's what I am after. Mr Damien Vanderbilt owns this media empire. He would be keen to run for president himself.

James:

- Revealing the truth could cause the opposition to win. We wouldn't want that.

Geoffrey:

- Damien is quite content with losing the presidency to Barry O'Connor. But he would rather give it a shot than allowing Mitchell Cent to run for president again.

James:

- And what if he loses to Eva Moreno?

Geoffrey:

- Eva Moreno doesn't stand a chance. It's impossible for someone who is neither Republican nor Democrat to become America's president.

James:

- It is not against the constitution and it can happen. That is something we ought to stop.

Beep, Beep, Beep

James Winter got distracted when his Zetan Monocle warned for danger. James got up, turned his back to Geoffrey and inserted the Zetan Monocle into his right eye. He squinted from discomfort as the monocle attached itself to his optical nerve, but it was a necessary evil. The monocle was the most intelligent AI on the planet, and James would be a fool to ignore this.

James' perception of time slowed down, as the Zetan Monocle displayed the following message:

'High threat level: Dozens of assailants from GAG, the Guns Against Globalism terrorist group have entered the building. Their objective seems to be acquiring the proof of the lethality of Reversogene. Suggested action: Destroy the security camera, subdue Geoffrey Bucker, steal the hard drive with stored evidence, and leave via the ventilation shaft. Probability of survival is 98 %, probability of success is 95%. Alternative options: Combat mode chance of winning is 72 %, Diplomacy mode 78 %'.

James resumed time and he chose the suggested action. He wouldn't risk his life to save Geoffrey, who supported another candidate than him. James pulled up his silenced pistol, shot the security camera, roundhouse kicked Geoffrey in the head, and picked up the laptop. James aimed his pistol, shot the hinges that held up the cover for the ventilation shaft, and got into the shaft.

There were a loud explosion and lots of gunfire. James set his monocle to 'avoid confrontation mode' and a hologram map of the air ventilation ducts came up in front of his right eye, guiding him to safety.

JAMES WINTER WAS BACK in his hotel room, a few blocks away from the FNN Headquarters. James had escaped before the SWAT team had stormed the building to fight the GAG terrorists. This was for the best. He didn't want anyone to know about his visit there, and he would need to tie up loose ends before the end of the day. James was examining Geoffrey's computer when he received a message from Pierre. The message read: 'Do you know anything about this?'

James opened the link. The link opened a video showing how GAG terrorists tortured and executed Geoffrey Bucker and other FNN executives. James felt a short burst of guilt. He could have stopped this from happening if he had accepted a 28 per cent probability of death and fought the terrorists.

James brushed off the guilt. Why would he risk his life to save those vultures on the executive level of FNN? Death was a suitable punishment for their deceit, and besides, they had proven to be uncooperative.

James had a bigger problem than guilt. He could not find the evidence about the lethality of the Reversogene drug. That proof could never see the light of the day, otherwise, Pierre would fall, and he would drag James with him. But where could the evidence be? James had hoped that it would be stored in Geoffrey's computer, but the Zetan Monocle had failed detecting it. Apparently, not even a genius alien AI could know everything.

James decided to come clean to Pierre. Pierre had real resources and Vladimir as an ally. These factors would make him better at finding and destroying the evidence than James. James wrote the following message:

'I couldn't find the evidence against us on Geoffrey's computer. I need help from your side. I will tie up some loose ends in New York.'

Pierre responded with:

- I will send Vladimir to have a chat with the GAG leader, Julienne Bessange. You can go back to playing stepdad for now. Be ready when I need you.

James sighed. He hated that Pierre was spying on him, but it was to be expected. Besides, he wasn't better himself, as the privacy of others were a danger to men that wanted to dominate the world.

Chapter 2: Pierre sends Vladimir to deal with the GAG leader Julienne Bessange, 10th June 2028.

It was a sunny Sunday afternoon, and Pierre Beaumont was sipping XO cognac on his terrace overlooking Lake Geneva from the top of a beautiful hill. He was annoyed that James Winter had failed to find and destroy the evidence for the adverse health effects of Reversogene. Sometimes, having the CIA director on his payroll was insufficient to convert inconvenient truths into forgotten falsehoods. However, Pierre knew who to send when James had failed. He would send his Siberian right-hand-man, Vladimir Kravchenko.

Pierre, Vladimir, and James were all members of the Monocle Conspiracy. The Monocle Conspiracy was not united by a single cause but by a single technology. In 2020, a group of nine individuals had found alien technology that elevated their minds while hiking in Nepal. The technology was in the form of a monocle that elevated the mind of the individual and made the wearer superior. The monocle allowed Pierre to anticipate future outcomes, and it enabled Vladimir to become the world's most dangerous assassin.

Pierre recalled the last meeting within the monocle conspiracy. The group had gathered in Colombia in February 2026 to find another Zetan Temple. They had hoped to unearth more marvellous technologies. Pierre had left Vladimir at home to avoid arousing the anger of Sandra Santiago, whose father Vladimir had murdered in Nepal. The mission in Colombia had been a fiasco, and Pierre had almost died when Zetan sentry bots had defended the temple. Worse yet, they had not found anything of value in the secret temple.

Pierre thought of assembling the Monocle Conspiracy again. It had been two years, and it was nice to meet with a group of people that shared the same experience and the same elevated mindsets.

Apart from Pierre, the other members of the Monocle Conspiracy were the following:

Vladimir Kravchenko was a sadistic Russian killer. Vladimir carried out assassinations for Pierre to fulfil his murderous desires. In return, Pierre used his wealth and influence to cover Vladimir's back, if he left incriminating evidence behind. Pierre and Vladimir had been occasional lovers over the years, but Pierre had left that part behind him. Vladimir was too dangerous, and Pierre did not intend to end his days, falling victim to a sadomasochistic sex marathon.

James Winter was the CIA director and the true power behind Mitchell Cent's presidency. Having the US president in his pocket was useful, and bribing the CIA director was less conspicuous than bribing the president.

Ben Yehuda & Szymon Yehuda were fanatic Zionists working for the Mossad. They wanted to commit genocide on non-Jews in Israel to fulfil a Zionist golden age dream. Pierre had funded these two brothers and their resurgence of the Templar Order, as they were too dangerous to be against him.

Martin Orchard was the man who had led the group to find the Zetan Monocles back in 2020. Martin was rash, unpredictable and dangerous. Pierre did not understand how Martin could be alive, after having returned from the dead several times. However, Martin was too fascinating to have Vladimir put him down permanently. Instead, Pierre had convinced the Yehuda Brothers to make Martin the leader of the resurgent Templar Order. Martin had gone missing in 2026 and Pierre had been too busy with his other schemes to find out about Martin's whereabouts.

Elaine Orchard was a middle-aged Indonesian business tycoon and Martin's estranged wife. Pierre had lent Elaine a fortune to make sure that her corporation, the Harapan Conglomerate, became the most powerful entity in South East Asia. Elaine's debts to Pierre made her controllable.

Josefina Fiero was a Brazilian femme fatale and business tycoon in her late 40's. Like Elaine's situation, Pierre had lent Josefina a fortune after the Hei Bai virus outbreak in 2021 had made him the wealthiest man on the planet. With Josefina indebted to him, her Avanço Verde-Ouro Corporation became the most powerful entity in South America.

Sandra Santiago was a pretty girl who was in her late teens. After Vladimir murdered Sandra's father in Nepal, Josefina took her in and raised her as her own.

Having contacted the members of the Monocle Conspiracy, Pierre went inside to have an afternoon nap.

WHEN PIERRE WOKE UP, Vladimir stood silent in the room, staring at him. Pierre sighed:

- I hope you didn't hurt my guards.

Vladimir scoffed:

- Hah. I wouldn't do that to you. I know how difficult it is to find good employees these days.

Pierre:

- So, how did you get in this time?

Vladimir:

- I climbed the mountainside. It's a nice challenging climb. It's the perfect warm-up for bed.

Pierre sighed. He lived in a palace on the top of a hill to avoid unannounced visitors, not to encourage them to climb the hill for fitness. Pierre:

- This is not a booty call, Vladimir. I summoned you for a new mission.

Vladimir:

- I love going on missions. Especially if they entail death and mayhem.

Pierre:

- I leave that to your discretion. I need you to confront the Guns against Globalist leader, Julienne Bessange. She has information about our involvement in the Hei Bai Virus outbreak and about the Reversogene cure that we created.

Vladimir:

- I like this mission already. I have seen the videos of what she can do with a gun. I bet that she would rock the bedroom!

Pierre:

- I don't think seduction is your strongest suit. Stick to your strengths.

Vladimir:

- I will stick to my strengths, but I will fuck her, and you cannot stop me. I will carry out the mission the way I like.

Pierre sighed. It would be a complication if Vladimir, the sex-crazed bisexual, raped Julienne during the mission. But the main goal was that Vladimir destroyed the evidence against them regarding Reversogene causing death and infertility. For minor crimes like rape and murder, Pierre could pay off the authorities for cover ups, especially if the rape victim was a well-known terrorist and a wanted criminal.

Pierre:

- Very well. Do what you deem necessary but don't leave too much of a mess.

Vladimir:

- Of course. I will keep the scene clean. I will find Julienne for you and I'll report back once I have completed the mission.

Pierre:

- Great. Please leave via the front door. I can't have you die in a climbing accident. Stopping Julienne is far too important.

Hearing this, Vladimir smirked, ran towards the ledge, and jumped off the cliff. Pierre looked towards the ledge and stared at Vladimir who plunged towards the ground, opening his parachute in the last moment. "Merde, bloody idiot!" Pierre mumbled to himself as he returned inside.

Chapter 3: Vladimir ends up in a coma, 18th June 2028.

Vladimir Kravchenko stood outside a shoddy farmhouse in rural Tennessee. Using his persuasion skills and force, mostly force, he had located Julienne Bessange's hideout. James Winter had told him that all police agencies in the USA were looking for Julienne after the attack on the FNN Headquarters, 12 days earlier. It was imperative that Vladimir found her first. If Julienne got captured, she could use the evidence against him and Pierre, to strike a deal with the authorities.

Vladimir scanned the building with his Zetan Monocle. The monocle revealed that there was only one person inside the building. This surprised Vladimir, but it also allowed him to fulfil his desires towards Julienne. This would have been far more difficult if armed men surrounded her.

Before entering the building, Vladimir noticed something interesting. A custom-made luxury car made in Indonesia. Indonesian cars weren't sold in America, so how had it got there? He walked up to the luxury car and he checked it out. He recognized the model, he had travelled in this exact car, a few years earlier, when Pierre had told him to be Elaine Orchard's bodyguard for a summit in the USA. But why was the car here, and what was the connection between Elaine and Julienne? Vladimir decided to focus on the mission. Once Julienne Bessange was dead and the evidence secured, Vladimir could discuss Elaine's car with Pierre. For now, it was crucial to focus on the mission.

Vladimir chose a stealthy approach and he entered the building. He made his way upstairs to the room where Julienne's heat signal came from.

Beep, Beep, Beep

Vladimir's monocle beeped to warn him of danger, but it was too late, as a bullet shot through his hand. He dropped the pistol in shock, and he turned to his right. What he saw amazed him. Covered in wet mud, Julienne was aiming her pistol at him. Vladimir smiled, he had never been outsmarted before and this strangely aroused him.

Vladimir:

- So, I guess you are not alone, after all?

Julienne:

- I am. What you see in the bed is a life-size doll with artificial heating that emulates my body heat to trick the infrared sensor in your monocle. I have been expecting you, Vladimir.

Vladimir:

- So, what do you know about me?

Julienne:

- You are Vladimir Kravchenko, the world's most ruthless assassin. I guess that Pierre Beaumont sent you.

Vladimir nodded and replied:

- You seem to have it all figured out.

Julienne:

- Yes, we are freedom fighters, not goons that Pierre Beaumont can bribe.

Vladimir:

- So, why am I still alive?

Julienne:

- I need you. The attack on the FNN Headquarters was our desperate attempt at taking down the treachery that rules the world. But they are fighting back, and we are losing. You are part of the Monocle Conspiracy, but Pierre is using you as a tool.

- Besides, I can offer you something that he can't.

Vladimir:

- What are you offering?

Julienne:

- Great sex and a challenging mission. Taking down the rest of the Monocle Conspiracy would be your greatest achievement!

Vladimir nodded and replied:

- You got me. I'll serve you if you spare me.

Julienne:

- Prove it to me. Take off your monocle and hand it to me."

Vladimir did as Julienne commanded, and he threw the monocle to her. Julienne studied the monocle for a while and almost put it on. Vladimir hoped that she would, as the Monocle would kill any unauthorised user. Instead, Julienne shocked Vladimir when she shot him in the leg. He groaned as he collapsed to the floor.

Julienne:

- You failed the test, Vladimir. The monocle would have killed me if I inserted it into my eye, yet you said nothing.

Vladimir:

- Hmph, funny that you knew about that. Did you expect me to change my loyalties at gunpoint?

Julienne:

- I could have given you everything. But now, all you'll receive is death!

Hearing this, Vladimir leapt towards Julienne. However, his injuries slowed him down, so she stopped him dead in his tracks with several bullets from her pistol. Getting shot in the chest, Vladimir stumbled a few steps backwards and fell out through a window.

———————————————

KABOOM

Julienne didn't have the chance to hear the bullet from James Winter's sniper rifle that ended her life. After shooting Julienne from afar, James rushed towards the farmhouse, accompanied by a few CIA operatives. He told his associates to rush Vladimir to the hospital, while he entered the farmhouse and secured Vladimir's monocle. While James found Vladimir's monocle, he could not find the evidence Julienne held against Pierre. Frustrated over this, James slammed the door and left the scene in anger.

Chapter 4: Trouble in the Campaign, 23rd June 2028.

It was early morning, and the sun was rising in the northeast. President Mitchell Cent was sitting in front of the large crucifix that he had erected on the Rose Garden lawn at the White House. This was the best time of the day. Mitchell was almost alone, and he felt close to God. This was a feeling he could not get later in his hectic days as the president of the United States. Mitchell planned to become a piece of history through being the longest-serving president in USA's presidential saga.

Mitchell had replaced President Deidrick Dump who had died in the Hei Bai Virus outbreak in 2021. According to the constitution, Mitchell was ineligible to run again. However, with the help of God, and some rich benefactors, he had found a loophole to circumvent the term limit. Mitchell transported his mind into a state of trance and he almost reached the Holy Ghost when one of his Secret Service agents interrupted him:

- Mr President. Mr Damien Vanderbilt is here to see you.

Mitchell:

- Of course. Please bring him to me, Joseph.

As Joseph walked away, Mitchell felt puzzled. Damien was his biggest sponsor and they met frequently, but the timing was off. Why was the media mogul Damien Vanderbilt visiting him at 5 in the morning? How could he know that Mitchell would be awake this early? The whole occurrence was absurd. Damien approached Mitchell and spoke:

- Greetings, Mitchell. I trust that you found God this morning. Early bird gets the worm, after all.

Mitchell:

- Yes. Early morning prayers are the best solace. But why are you here? You haven't booked an appointment and you're visiting at a time when few would be awake.

Damien:

- I wanted to be away from the prying eyes of the press. I have some important matters to discuss.

Mitchell:

- You own the prying eyes of the press. They will never bite the hand that feeds them.

Damien:

- I own most but not all news and social media. One can never be too careful.

Mitchell:

- So, what do you wish to discuss?

Damien:

- The upcoming presidential election.

Mitchell:

- What's new? Thank you for rigging the Democrat's primaries so that I am facing the senile idiot Barry O'Connor. This will be a walk in the park.

Damien:

- Yes, but not for you, Mitchell.

Mitchell:

- What do you mean, Damien?

Damien:

- I came to tell you that I have decided to take your spot in the election. I have made my money. Now I want my shot at the presidency.

Mitchell:

- Are you out of your mind? You helped me winning the primaries and now you want me gone? That doesn't make any sense!

Damien:

- It makes more sense than your stupid Bronze Age biblical belief. I wanted you to win so I could take your place. Winning the primaries would have been difficult. Convincing you to step down will be a piece of cake.

Mitchell:

- I don't think so. I will run for president without your support if I have to. I'll defeat Barry without your help.

Damien:

- Not when the population finds out about your involvement in the Reversogene cover-up. They'll vote you out and you'll go to jail. This is the evidence Guns against Globalism was looking for when they attacked the FNN Headquarters. Fortunately, I had already moved the evidence before my mole convinced them to attack one of my TV stations.

Damien handed Mitchell the documents proving his claim. Mitchell stared at the documents in terror, unsure on how to proceed. Eventually, Mitchell spoke:

- So, what do you want? Why did you convince GAG to attack your own TV station?

Damien:

- I already told you what I want. I want your spot in the presidential election.

- As for orchestrating the GAG attack on the FNN, I had several motives. Firstly, the attack got rid of Geoffrey Bucker for me. I have wanted to fire him for a long time, but I worried over what evidence he has against me. GAG solved this pickle for me. Secondly, I wanted to drag GAG out in the open. After the attack, they have become the public enemy number one. Besides, their backing by the Chinese government doesn't strengthen their claim to be civil liberty fighters.

Mitchell:

- I see. It seems that you have it all figured out. So, if I comply with your terms, how do I give you my spot in the presidential election?

Damien:

- You'll blame your withdrawal on illness and your religious fervour, which demands your full focus on God. But don't worry about that for now. I'll brief you on what to say and when to say it before we'll make the public announcement.

- I need to head to my private jet. God bless you, President Cent.

Mitchell didn't reply and he watched how Damien Vanderbilt entered his car that drove him away from the White House. Mitchell sighed. He was in a mess, but there was also some silver lining to it. At least, he knew who held the evidence against him for the Reversogene cover-up.

Mitchell called James Winter to have the situation rectified.

James answered the phone in confusion since Mitchell woke him up:

- Hmm, President Cent. What is going on? Has something happened?

Mitchell:

- Damien Vanderbilt holds incriminating evidence against us. We need to deal with him, immediately. Oh, and allegedly China is funding Guns against Globalism.

James:

- When you say deal with him, you mean...?

Mitchell:

- How we normally deal with threats against national security. That evidence must never see the light of day.

James:

- Okay. I'll drive to the White House so we can discuss this. Don't make any rash moves, President Cent.

James Winter got out of bed and headed to his car. He knew that killing Damien Vanderbilt would be a disastrous move that could ruin everything. James needed to discuss this with Pierre before acting on President Cent's orders. Filled with doubts, James entered his car to drive the long way to the White House.

Chapter 5: Cloaks and Daggers in Indonesia, 24th June 2028.

Min Li, the former mistress of the late Chairman Jing Xi, smiled at the stern-looking Budi Sepulyat, who was the Head of Security of the Indonesian Harapan Conglomerate. Min Li felt terrified and she prayed that she could convince Budi to let her leave the Harapan Conglomerate Headquarters.
Budi:

- Miss Li. Where are you going?

Min:

- I am going to lunch.

Budi listened to a message in his headset and then he responded:

- Lunch sounds good. I am coming with you.

Min:

- Oh. I'd love to, but I have a date with someone else.

Budi scoffed:

- Bah. I AM coming with you for lunch. Would you rather come with me to the security office?

Min:

- Lunch is fine. I am sure my date won't mind.

Budi:

- I am sure he will understand.

- Let's go to the Pempek Bali restaurant across the street. I have heard they have great Gado-Gado salad.

Min nodded and forced a smile. She felt terrified. She had a USB memory with evidence that she had stolen from Elaine Orchard's office. The last thing she wanted to do was to have lunch with Elaine's terrifying beefed-up body-guard.

They crossed the street in silence and got seated at the restaurant. A waitress arrived at their table and Budi ordered:

- Dua Gado Gado, ekstra pedas. Buat mereka cepat, aku tidak punya waktu seharian! *(Two Gado-gado, extra spicy. Make them quick, I don't have all day!)*

The waitress seemed a bit offended by Budi's commanding tone, but she nodded and rushed off.

Min:

- You don't need to be rude to the attendants, Budi.

Budi:

- Bah, time is money. I don't have all day. That's why I'll cut straight to the point.

- Why were you in Mistress Elaine's office?

Min:

- I was looking for her. I wanted to present my latest artwork.

Budi:

- You should have booked an appointment instead of stealing my access card.

Min:

- I am sorry. Harapan is a huge company and I wanted to get ahead of my competition.

Budi:

- Can you promise me I won't find anything incriminating if I check through your handbag?

Saying this, Budi grabbed Min's handbag and opened it. Min put her hand on Budi's hand, looked him straight into his eyes, and pleaded:

- Please, Budi. You must trust me. I'll do anything to please you.

Budi looked at Min Li's beautiful Chinese eyes with his heart full of desire. He licked his lips and replied:

- There is a hotel around the corner. I don't need to be at work for a couple of hours.

Min Li swallowed her shock. The mission was too important, and she feared Budi would kill her if she did not play along with his games. Besides, Budi was considered attractive compared to the fat and disgusting Chairman Jing Xi, she had been the unwilling mistress to, until Jing Xi's death in 2021. Min Li responded with a fake excitement:

- Oh, hee-hee. I like what you are suggesting. I also have a few hours to kill.

Hearing this, Budi smiled and showed off a few missing teeth and a golden grill. He walked up to the counter, left a couple of hundred thousand Rupiahs to pay for the food, and led Min away from the establishment.

EILEEN LU WAS RESTING in the presidential suite of the Manhattan Hotel in Jakarta. She had discussed a new trade deal with the Indonesian president, and she hoped this deal could restart China's struggling economy. She had to get the economy started, as a presidential election was looming in China, and the people were getting restless.

The collapse of the Columnist Party of China (CPOC) in 2021 had destroyed China's economy. Eileen Lu had destroyed the prospects of economic recovery when she refused to be the puppet president of the corporate giants. Eileen Lu standing up to the corporations had initially been immensely popular in China. For the first time in history, China had leadership that embraced the unique Chinese culture as well as civil rights and democracy. Riding on a wave of popularity from her reforms as an interim president, Eileen Lu had won a decisive victory in the 2023 presidential election.

Despite her successes, Eileen Lu was in serious trouble. After becoming the president and refusing to sell out Chinese assets to the World Bank, her former allies at the World Bank had turned hostile and put China under economic warfare. This in combination with the fighting that surrounded the regime change had brought China to the brink of financial ruin. The people who were used to an improving economy were angry with Eileen and she couldn't silence them. Silencing dissenters would make her the same evil that she had fought. Hence, securing a trade deal with Indonesia and improving the economy was Eileen's last chance at winning the 2028 Chinese election.

There was a knock on the door, and Eileen's bodyguard spoke:

- Mrs President Lu. You have a visitor requesting to meet with you. It's Min Li, the former Mistress of Chairman Xi.

Eileen Lu nodded and replied:

- Okay. Bring her in a couple of minutes.

Eileen closed the door and she turned on the kettle. She would drink the special tea variety her herbalist had composed. It was an exclusive blend that Empress Wu Zetian had developed during her reign, a blend that had been forgotten for over 1000 years. Eileen Lu had a sip of the tea and she smiled. The flavour was divine.

There was another knock on the door and Min Li entered the suite. Eileen studied Min Li. While Eileen's middle-aged beauty had faded somewhat from the stress of being China's president, Min was still a stunning beauty in her prime age. At first, Eileen had disliked Min Li, as she was Chairman Jing Xi's mistress. But when they had met face to face, Eileen had realised that they had experienced a comparable situation. Min Li had been repulsed by Jing Xi, but she had rather accepted his advances than risk getting raped and killed by the power-hungry tyrant, and having her entire family murdered.

Eileen looked at Min Li again. Her eyes were teary, and her body was shaking. Eileen walked up to Min, comforted her, and spoke softly:

- Darling, what happened? Did my guards mistreat you?

Min:

- I feel so dirty. I had to have sex with him, or he would have found out about our plan, and he would have killed me. He was so rough and disrespectful to me.

Eileen:

- Who is he?

Min:

- Budi Sepulyat, the Head of Security at the Harapan Conglomerate and Elaine Orchard's watchdog.

Eileen:

- Tell me what happened?

Min:

- I snuck into Elaine's office with a swipe key that I stole from Budi. I downloaded secret documents proving that the Harapan Conglomerate sponsored Guns against Globalism and made it look like our country was behind it.

- Budi found out, and he threatened to expose me unless I had sex with him.

Eileen:

- I see. Do you have these documents?

Min:

- Of course. That's why I hurried here. You're the president of China, I oblige to what you ask me to do.

After saying this, Min handed Eileen a USB drive. She inserted the drive into a laptop and opened the documents that proved her claim.
Eileen studied the files for a while and spoke:

- It seems that we must leave Indonesia at once. If the Harapan Conglomerate wants to harm China, it is not safe for us here anymore. You better join me, Min Li.

Min nodded:

- Thank you. I am sorry if the news is damaging the trade agreement.

Eileen:

- Well, it's better to not have an agreement than signing a trade deal with the enemy. You better stay in the guestroom. I'll organise a swift return to China for the two of us.

Min:

- Thank you. I would like to take a shower now.

Eileen:

- Of course. The bathroom is over there.

After hearing this, Min Li had a long shower where she scrubbed herself hard after the unfortunate rendezvous with Budi. Meanwhile, Eileen gathered her ministers to discuss the matter and plan for how to leave Indonesia immediately.

'WAS THE SEX ENJOYABLE?' Elaine Orchard smirked cunningly. She knew that Budi desired Min Li's beauty, and when she had realised that Min Li was a spy, Elaine would let Budi fulfil his desires.

Budi:

- It was great. She is an extraordinary beauty.

Elaine:

- Tsk, tsk, Budi. When are you going to find a woman who is not terrified by you?

- Anyway, everything went according to plan. So, thank you, Budi.

Budi:

- But I don't understand this, Mistress. Why did you instruct me to have sex with her and let her go? Now China knows that we are funding Guns against Globalism.

Elaine:

- Tsk, tsk. Are you complaining after having sex with the woman of your wet dreams?

Budi:

- Of course not. I was simply curious about your plan.

Elaine:

- The sex was to reward you, and to test her. Now I know that she is a spy that would do anything to complete her mission for her Chinese president, Ms Eileen Lu.

- But in saying this, I won. The document I allowed her to copy contained a virus that infected Eileen's computer. My spies are listening to the Chinese leaders as we speak. They told me that Eileen and Min Li are paranoid, and they are going to leave Indonesia.

- Eileen abandoning the upcoming trade meeting will insult our Indonesian president Fadhlan Azim. This will further the crisis in China, which will please Pierre.

- As for me, I will offer President Azim a better deal, which will bring us closer. This is a big win in just one day.

Budi:

- I see. Shall I kill Min Li for betraying us?

Elaine:

- No. Her betrayal was exactly what we needed. Besides, I assume the sex with you was punishment enough? Ha-ha!

Budi smirked but didn't say anything. Elaine spoke again:

- Now leave, I need to rest after a good day's work.

As Budi left, Elaine picked up her phone and messaged Pierre Beaumont:

- It's done. I have made sure that Eileen abandons the trade meeting with President Azim. I will put in a good word for your proposal to open a uranium mine in Aceh.

After doing this, Elaine leaned back into her chair, and she summoned a masseuse to massage her feet. A 3-hour massage and a bottle of expensive red wine was the perfect end to a productive day.

Chapter 6: Pierre visits the comatose Vladimir, 25th June 2028.

Pierre Beaumont exited his private jet in Washington. He worried about Vladimir Kravchenko, who had been in a coma since his confrontation with Julienne Bessange one week earlier. This worry annoyed him. Vladimir was just a tool to further his goals, by far his best tool, but still only one out of many. Pierre shed a tear. Did he still have feelings for Vladimir, after all? Pierre had been terrified of Vladimir's capabilities since the New York Hei Bai Virus outbreak in 2021.

In 2021, Pierre had intended to kill the world leaders at the UN summit to crash the world markets. But Vladimir had gone beyond Pierre's order and spread the virus across New York City, instead of killing only the world leaders at the summit, causing over 300,000 unwarranted deaths. After this, Pierre had realised that he and Vladimir were incompatible as partners, but Pierre had kept Vladimir close for his skills, and because the alternative, which was to be Vladimir's enemy, terrified Pierre.

James Winter met Pierre at the tarmac of the airport. James smirked and taunted Pierre:

- Have you been watching melodramatic movies again, Pierre?

Pierre:

- What are you talking about?

James:

- You are crying.

Pierre:

- Mon Dieu. It's my bloody hay fever.

James:

- Whatever you say. I picked up Vladimir's monocle from the GAG hideout. You'll need a new agent to wear it.

Having said this, James handed Vladimir's monocle to Pierre. Pierre looked at it for a while, nodded, and spoke:

- Yet, I don't know how to reprogram the monocle to a new user. The monocles tend to be lethal to non-authorised users. Such a mess and such a waste!

- Anyway, where is Vladimir? I would like to see him.

James:

- He is at the National Military Hospital. But there is no point. He is brain dead. I had to pull some strings to keep the respirator going. He is a foreign national with a fake ID after all.

Pierre:

- I see. I'll bring him back to Switzerland. I'll find a way to save him. If a Zeto Crystal brought Martin Orchard back to life, it can also bring back Vladimir.

James:

- Whatever you say, Pierre. Get in the car and I'll take you to the hospital.

After saying this, James and Pierre entered an armoured limousine. James Winter remembered President Cent's request to kill Damien Vanderbilt. He was against the idea, but he needed to discuss it with Pierre. James Winter cleared his throat and spoke:

- There has been a development regarding the upcoming presidential election.

Pierre:

- Oh really. Is Mitchell Cent unwilling to concede his presidential spot to Damien Vanderbilt?

James:

- Worse. He tasked me with killing Damien.

Pierre:

- That is unacceptable. Damien is one of my closest business partners, while Mitchell is a fool. Convince him to resign.

James:

- How do I do this?

Pierre:

- The monocle records all your interactions. Access the recorded conversation where Mitchell tasked you to kill Damien, transfer it to a portable hard drive, and show the video to Mitchell's chief of staff, Elise Santos. She will convince him to resign.

James:

- And what do I do if Mitchell targets me?

Pierre:

- Then you are allowed to kill him. But I want to keep the presidential assassinations to a minimum. It's too messy, unless you have a narrative to feed the people.

James:

- Understood, Pierre.

Pierre nodded and he closed his eyes while the limousine took them to the military hospital where Vladimir was in a coma.

PIERRE ENTERED THE hospital ward, where Vladimir was attached to a respirator. Pierre concluded that the technology in the room was obsolete, and he felt angry that Vladimir wasn't given better care. Then again, to the Americans, Vladimir was just an unidentified thug and not the most valuable operative of the world's richest man. Pierre had kept his association with Vladimir as secret as possible. It suited them better. For Pierre, the advantage was that he could claim innocence if Vladimir was caught. For Vladimir, the advantage had been that he was less recognisable when he was outside of the spotlight, which decreased the risk of him getting caught.

Pierre walked up to the comatose Vladimir, pushed him gently, and exclaimed:

- Vladimir! Wake up you big Russian bear. I know you can hear me.

Vladimir didn't respond to the touch or to Pierre's shrill voice. Pierre felt how desperation was taking hold of him. He had hoped that this would be one of Vladimir's morbid jokes, where Vladimir would spring up from the dead with a thundering laughter. This did not happen, and sorrow overwhelmed Pierre. Pierre's voice broke, and he snivelled:

- Vladimir. Please wake up. I know that I never told you, but I have feelings for you. I also fear you, but I will do everything to bring you back to life. I need to visit Elaine Orchard and find that idiotic ex-husband of her, Martin Orchard. If Martin could come back from the dead, so can you.

Hearing this, the unconscious Vladimir made a bit of sound. Pierre noticed this and spoke:

- Is Martin Orchard the key to bringing you back, Vladimir?

Vladimir remained silent, and Pierre tried again:

- Is Elaine Orchard the key to what happened to you?

Vladimir growled again, and Pierre understood that he needed to seek out Elaine to find out what her involvement was. Pierre left the room to speak to James Winter:

- Elaine Orchard must be involved in what happened to Vladimir.

James:

- Are you sure? She hasn't been to America for over a year.

Pierre:

- I doubt she travels herself to get things done. Can you check the whereabouts of her two closest men, Budi and Rexi?

James:

- Hmm. You might be right. There was an Indonesian-made car at the farm where Julienne Bessange shot Vladimir. But that car was registered as stolen.

Pierre:

- Why would Julienne steal a Harapan Conglomerate car if they weren't involved with her? I will need to discuss this matter with Elaine.

James:

- Okay. What do you want me to do?

Pierre:

- My lawyers will contact the Department of Justice requesting that they send Vladimir to our care-facility in Switzerland. I need you to make sure there are no legal problems with that request.

James:

- Understood. I'll contact you if the need arises.

Pierre nodded and walked away. He would need to find a way to bring Vladimir back to life, but first he needed to make sure that Elaine fell back in line. He had sponsored the Harapan Conglomerate with billions of dollars from his ill-gotten Hei Bai Virus outbreak windfall, and she shouldn't keep him in the dark.

Pierre reached his car and he turned to his personal assistant, Jean Valmont:

- I need you to organise a meeting with Indonesia's president, Mr Fadhlan Azim.

Jean:

- Of course, Monsieur Beaumont. When would you like me to book the meeting?

Pierre:

- Tomorrow. We are flying there today.

Jean:

- I don't understand, Pierre. Why haven't you mentioned this before? Has something happened?

Pierre felt irritated that Jean had the audacity to question his orders, but he decided to not act on his irritation. Jean's performance held an acceptable standard and she had served him for seven years. Getting another dimwit to replace her would only cause him more headaches.

Pierre:

- China pulled out from the trade meeting with Indonesia. I need to discuss the repercussions with President Azim. Besides, Indonesia owes me a lot of money, and he should beckon at my calling.

Jean:

- Understood, Monsieur Beaumont.

Pierre nodded and turned to the driver:

- Take us to the airport.

After that he entered the car and sat in silence.

PIERRE WAS ON HIS PRIVATE jet, and he tried to ignore Jean's annoying voice so he could enjoy his glass of red wine in peace. Meeting with President Azim was a diversion from Pierre's real goal in Indonesia, which was to confront Elaine Orchard about her connection with Guns against Globalism. However, it would seem very strange if Pierre visited Indonesia without meeting President Azim, since Eileen Lu's abandonment of the trade discussions had made worldwide headlines.

Pierre felt how his headache was getting worse. Listening to Jean's briefing was like hearing nails on a chalkboard, and Pierre wanted peace and quiet more than anything. While he could tell her to shut up, there was better ways of keeping her from talking.

In the last few years, Pierre had occasionally requested fellatio services from Jean. While he didn't particularly enjoy her talents, or the fact that she was a woman, he enjoyed the power he felt from fucking his secretary. Pierre turned to Jean and spoke:

- Enough of the briefing, Jean. I am tired and I need to relax. There are better ways for you to use your mouth.

Having said this, Pierre tilted his seat back, while pointing at his crotch. Jean hesitated for a bit but eventually gave in to Pierre's request.

As Jean gave Pierre fellatio, he sighed of relief. Most of all, he was relieved that he didn't have to suffer listening to her voice anymore. After finishing, Pierre took a sleeping pill, flushed it down with red wine, and fell asleep with a smug grin on his face.

Chapter 7: Mitchell Cent concedes his spot in the Presidential Election to Damien Vanderbilt, 26th June 2028.

James Winter was waiting outside the oval office. He had booked an appointment with President Cent's chief of staff, Ms Elise Santos. James worried about the meeting, as there were two possible negative outcomes. Either Elise wouldn't believe him, or she would believe him but decide to silence him instead. James shook off his fears. With the Zetan Monocle inserted, he would be difficult to kill, although Vladimir had fallen a few days earlier, proving that the monocle did not make the user invincible.

Elise entered the waiting room and she approached James. James studied her as she entered. She was a Latina woman in her fifties. Like a large portion of the American population, she hadn't looked after herself, and she was sporting a "Type 2 diabetes" body shape. James pushed his judgemental thoughts aside and he forced a smile as he spoke:

- Thanks for seeing me today, Secretary Santos.

Elise didn't reciprocate James' fake smile. Instead, she gave him a stern look and spoke:

- Stop wasting my time with that disingenuous smile, CIA Director Winter. Tell me why you are here.

James sighed. While it was a relief that he didn't need to smile at the hideous Elise, he had hoped that his attractive looks would help him convince her to see things his way.

James took out his phone, and he played a video recording where Mitchell tasked him with killing Damien Vanderbilt.

Elise gave James a sceptical look, and after a few seconds she replied:

- So, I assume that you are not interested in the mission President Cent offered you.

James:

- Thanks for stating the obvious. My associates and I would like Mitchell to concede his spot in the election to Damien Vanderbilt.

Elise:

- I see. I will notify President Cent about your request. Was there anything else, Director Winter?

James hesitated. He couldn't read Elise, and he damned himself for not wearing his monocle to assist him. James felt how his chest went tight, and his worried mind gave him visions of how Mitchell's thugs would kill Melinda and her children. '*Damn. I should have thought about Melinda's family's safety,*' James reflected.
James:

- That is all, Elise. Thank you for your time.

After saying this, James dragged himself to the closest toilet and he purged from his fear. '*I hope my visions are not real.*' James thought, pulled himself together, and left the Whitehouse.

PRESIDENT MITCHELL Cent was kneeling in front of the crucifix in the Oval Office when Elise Santos entered. Mitchell turned his head, gave her a disapproving look, and turned towards the crucifix again. Elise hesitated for a bit, cleared her throat, and spoke:

- President Cent, there has been a dangerous development.

Mitchell turned around and reprimanded Elise:

- You should never disturb me when I am connecting with God.

Elise:

- But President Cent, this is important.

Mitchell sighed and replied:

- Very well. Tell me what's on your mind, Elise.

Elise:

- I met with CIA director James Winter. He showed me a recorded conversation of how you tried to convince him to kill Damien Vanderbilt. He demands that you concede your spot in the upcoming election to Damien.

Mitchell looked at the recorded video and he swore to himself. He had misjudged James Winter. He had believed that James was a true patriot who would do anything for his country. Instead, it turned out that James was a lackey of Damien Vanderbilt, who supported that Swiss faggot Pierre Beaumont. Mitchell grabbed a vase, chucked it into the wall, and exclaimed:

- Damn those unbelievers! Damn them all! They are all enemies of God's work!

Elise:

- Who are they?

Mitchell:

- James Winter, Damien Vanderbilt, and Pierre Beaumont.

Elise:

- But aren't you close to all of them?

Mitchell:

- Not anymore. Can we kill them all?

Elise:

- Mr President. This is unconstitutional and I can't believe that you are suggesting it.

Mitchell sunk into his chair. He sighed and stared into his palms. Eventually, he spoke:

- You're right. Please call a press conference and ask Damien Vanderbilt to get here. I will concede my spot in the election to him.

Elise:

- Understood, President Cent. I will make all the necessary arrangements.

———————— ✕╫╁╫ ————————

LATER THE SAME DAY, Damien Vanderbilt arrived at the Whitehouse and met with Mitchell Cent before the press conference. Damien walked up to Mitchell and taunted:

- Thank you for conceding your spot to me, Mitchell. It would have been more worthwhile if you did so before considering killing me.

Mitchell grumbled:

- Wouldn't you have done the same thing, Damien?

Damien:

- Yes. But I am not hiding behind the will of God.

Mitchell:

- I know. Yet, to become the President of the USA, you must pretend to follow our saviour, like my predecessor Deidrick Dump did.

Damien:

- I am sure that I can partake in that ploy. Politics and religion are just stage performances for the masses. The real powerbrokers make the decisions behind the scenes. Even the Romans knew this.

Mitchell:

- Yes. So, what policies and ideologies are you planning to promote before the election?

Damien:

- I don't know yet. Policies don't interest me. All I care about is the power and wealth of my associates and I. But I know one thing, with my world-class campaign staff, it will be easy to defeat Barry O'Connor. He is senile and even his own party loathes him.

- Anyway, as much as I love chatting with you, we have a press conference to attend.

Mitchell nodded and the two men headed for the auditorium where the press had gathered.

MITCHELL CENT WAS CRYING in front of the Virgin Mary bronze figurine in his bedroom. Damien was the devil, and yet he had conceded his spot in the election to him. As Mitchell looked at the figurine through his teary eyes, it seemed to him that the statuette was weeping blood. He heard a peal of menacing hissing laughter in the back of his head and he threw the figurine at the bulletproof glass window. The figurine bounced and came back to hit Mitchell in the head, cutting his chin.

Elise Santos rushed in together with a few nurses. She jabbed Mitchell in the neck with a syringe. The last thing that Mitchell remembered before passing out was Elise urging the nurses:

- Take President Cent to the medical ward in our bunker. For the sake of our nation, this episode must not become public knowledge.

Chapter 8: Pierre Beaumont pulls Elaine Orchard back in line, 28th June 2028.

Pierre was visiting the ARTsphere Gallery in Jakarta. He was watching a Javanese gamelan performance, and the beautiful intricate musical notes were driving him crazy. He didn't have time for this, he needed to discuss the issues that Elaine Orchard had caused at once. Elaine had allowed a Chinese spy sent by Eileen Lu to infiltrate her computer database and steal priceless evidence against Pierre. The evidence proved that the drug Reversogene was more dangerous than the Hei Bai virus that it claimed to cure.

Pierre had built his absolute fortune from releasing the Hei Bai Virus, shorting the market, and then releasing the drug that cured the virus. While Eileen couldn't prove that Pierre released the Hei Bai Virus, the evidence of Reversogene's dangerous side effects could still ruin and discredit him. It was crucial that this evidence did not gain popular traction.

Pierre also needed to discuss whether Elaine had supported the Guns Against Globalism attack on the FNN Headquarters. Pierre needed to make sure that Elaine fell back in line and didn't make these decisions on her own. Pierre had made Elaine wealthy with his ill-gotten gains, and he expected loyalty.

As Pierre thought that his eardrums were about to burst from the music, Elaine approached him:

- Come, Pierre. I need you to make a bid on an antique sculpture at the auction next door.

Pierre nodded and followed Elaine to the next room. As he closed the door behind him, he felt relieved as he needed to divert his mind.

The auction was about to start, and Pierre whispered to Elaine:

- You have kept me waiting for several days. I don't appreciate waiting.

Elaine shrugged her shoulders and replied:

- I wanted you to take your time with President Fadhlan Azim. He should be an important dignitary for the CEO of the World Bank to meet.

Pierre scoffed:

- I didn't come to Indonesia to discuss charity and school projects in Aceh. I have more important matters to discuss with you.

- What is your connection to Guns against Globalism?

Elaine looked away, took a deep breath, sighed, and spoke:

- Please make a bid on this sculpture, Pierre. I will tell you afterwards.

Pierre nodded and he bid on the Balinese sculpture of the demoness Rangda. Much to his dismay, there was another prospective buyer and Pierre ended up in a bidding war. After ten minutes of bidding, Pierre lost his patience and he bid USD2,000,000. This move deterred his opponent and Pierre finally won the auction. Elaine nodded at Pierre and spoke:

- Thank you, Pierre. Follow me to a private dining room upstairs and I will tell you everything I know.

AS THEY GOT SEATED at the dining table, Pierre whinged:

- Why did you make me spend USD2,000,000 on that ugly sculpture?

Elaine:

- That sculpture was of the Demoness Rangda from Balinese mythology. Did you know my ex-husband believes Rangda is speaking to him via the monocle?

Pierre:

- Do I look like a person who doesn't know things? Of course, I know the origins of the Zetan monocles' power. I still don't know why you need that ugly sculpture. My Zetan monocle didn't give me any hints to its usefulness.

Elaine:

- I don't need it. That's why I sold it to you.

Pierre:

- Huh. Why would you sell me an ugly statue?

Elaine:

- Because I ran into some problems with my mining project at Taliabu Island. However, when my bank sees that this sculpture has sold for USD2,000,000; I can use my other 50 statuettes as security for a bank loan.

Pierre:

- I see. That is smart accounting.
- Now tell me about your connection to Guns Against Globalism.

Elaine ignored Pierre's question. She picked up a bakso beef meatball from the soup set menu with her chopsticks, slurped and said:

- These meatballs are divine. Do you want to try one?

Elaine didn't wait for Pierre's reply. She stuffed her mouth with the beef meatball and started chewing it, giving out a slight moan of pleasure as she enjoyed its meaty juices.

Pierre tapped the table in irritation, and after watching Elaine stuffing her face for a couple of minutes, he had enough. Pierre roared:

- Enough of this, Elaine. Tell me about your connection to Guns Against Globalism now!

Elaine nodded, swallowed her bakso and drank her soup, wiped her mouth with a napkin, and spoke.

- I met with Julienne Bessange a couple of months ago. She provided some evidence for Reversogene being a dangerous drug. I wanted to find out the truth, so I sponsored the GAG attack on the FNN Headquarters.

Pierre:

- Bah. The truth on Reversogene. What does it matter to you?

A tear ran down Elaine's chin and she sobbed:

- My niece died in 2022 after taking Reversogene. Julienne hinted that a lot of people had died from the drug and that Damien Vanderbilt was covering it up. I wanted the truth to come out.

Pierre hesitated. He wanted to scold Elaine for her stupidity that put them all in danger, but this was not the time nor the place. It was dangerous to taunt someone when they experienced grief. Besides, Indonesia was Elaine's backyard and the local law enforcement would take her side if there was a conflict. Pierre tried to use empathy to get out of this pickle and stop a dangerous situation from unfolding.

Pierre:

- I am sorry to hear that. I should have warned you about the dangerous side effects of Reversogene. I worried that the Global Health

Association wouldn't approve the drug if I disclosed the truth. If it wasn't for the Reversogene drug, the Hei Bai virus would ravage humanity.

Elaine nodded:

- Yes, I guess you are right. The Hei Bai virus outbreak was terrible. Thank you for saving us all.

Pierre exhaled. He was lucky that Elaine didn't know the truth about the Hei Bai Virus. When someone had been infected, the Hei Bai Virus only became active when these infected people ingested large doses of selenium, and thus it was easy to avoid negative effects. Pierre put a hand on Elaine's shoulder and spoke:

- Look. I feel guilty about what happened to your niece. How about I pay off your debts for the Taliabu Island project?

Elaine wiped her tears and smiled at Pierre:

- Thank you, but I already owe you a lot of money and I don't want to be in more debt.

Pierre smiled:

- Don't be silly. This is a chance for us to get a fresh start. I am willing to forgive all your debts so you can use your money to form Indonesia as you envision it.

Elaine:

- That's amazing. Thank you very much. I can't wait to make Indonesia the greatest nation on Earth.

Pierre:

- That's who I am. A generous soul keen to help.

- Considering the fortune that I am about to give you, will you help me make sure that Damien Vanderbilt wins the US presidential election? I need help to cover up the Reversogene debacle.

Elaine:

- I will help you. But you must promise to be forthcoming with me in the future.

'Yeah right!' Pierre thought, but he responded:

- Of course, Elaine. I promise.

Having said this, Pierre got up from the table and corrected his tie. Elaine gave him a confused look:

- Are you leaving? But you haven't eaten anything?

Pierre:

- You have to forgive me, but I am attending a state banquet with President Azim in two hours. You know how slow Jakarta traffic can be.

Pierre didn't wait for Elaine's response. Instead, he turned around and strode for the exit.

PIERRE SENT THE INDONESIAN ladyboy away from his hotel room after he had done his deeds, and he collapsed on his bed. While it felt good being the one on the top in Vladimir's absence, Pierre worried about his Russian assassin and sadomasochistic lover. Apart from his love of money, Vladimir was Pierre's next greatest love. However, Vladimir's aggressiveness also terrified Pierre, who worried about his life every time they met.

'Maybe it is better if Vladimir stays where he is.' Pierre muttered to himself. Pierre leaned back and closed his eyes. Exhausted from the intense meeting with Elaine Orchard and the sex with the ladyboy escort, Pierre fell asleep.

Chapter 9: Eileen Lu Releases Crucial Evidence to Eva Moreno, 10th July 2028.

Eva Luisa Moreno was waiting in anticipation in a villa located at the Yuanyang Terraced Fields in Southern China. The afternoon was hot and humid, but a slight breeze made it comfortable. Eva sighed. While she didn't mind spending some time holidaying in China, her time was too precious for such pursuits. Her worst nightmare for America was about to take place. The corrupt media tycoon, Damien Vanderbilt, had replaced Mitchell Cent as the Republican candidate after Mitchell had withdrawn his candidacy. Damien would defeat the senile Barry O'Connor in the upcoming US presidential election. Eva couldn't allow this scenario to happen. She loved her country and democracy too much to allow this disaster. She needed to win the election herself.

Eva's problem was that she didn't have a large party nor any wealthy supporters. Besides, no independent candidate had ever become the president in the past. Yet, after witnessing the ludicrous debate between Damien and Barry, Eva knew that she had to become the first independent president. During the debate, Barry had fallen over and forgotten what year it was. His candidacy was blatant proof that the electoral college in his party had sent an unelectable candidate. Damien's candidacy was equally suspicious. Just two weeks earlier, the incumbent president, Mitchell Cent, had conceded his spot in the election to Damien due to unknown reasons.

Eva knew that she had to act fast to save American democracy. Through a strange twist of fate, Chinese agents had promised her crucial information about Damien if she went with them to China. It had been an offer that she couldn't refuse, at least Eva had felt so when several armed Chinese agents approached her house. After twelve hours on a private jet, Eva had landed in

Southern China, fearful but confident about one thing. The Chinese agents didn't intend to kill her.

Eva sighed and took another sip of the exquisite tea the Chinese agents had served her. Whatever was about to happen, it was outside of her control, so she was better off living in the present. Eva cleared her mind and found inner peace as she enjoyed the beautiful views and a delicious blend of Chinese tea.

EILEEN LU:

  - Welcome to China, US Presidential candidate Eva Luisa Moreno.

Eva woke up from her thoughts and she stared at Eileen in awe. Why on Earth had the president of China, President Eileen Lu, come to see her?
Eileen smiled and she spoke again:

  - Oh, I am sorry, how rude of me to not introduce myself. I am President Eileen Lu of China.

Eva:

  - President Lu, what are you doing here?

Eileen:

  - I am here to talk to you. I am sorry I didn't extend a formal invitation. However, it is better for your chances in the upcoming election if our association is not made public.

Eva:

  - Your agents said that you have incriminating evidence against Damien Vanderbilt?

Eileen:

- I do. These classified reports prove that the Reversogene drug against the Hei Bai Virus killed a lot more people than the virus did. These reports can expose the top-secret scheme, which Pierre Beaumont and James Winter has been involved in. They are behind Reversogene, Damien Vanderbilt was using his media influence power to cover it up, and President Mitchell Cent was covering up their criminal conspiracy, which caused the deaths of millions of Americans.

Eva:

- These are severe accusations.

Eileen:

- Yes, and I urge you to do your own research. It is, however, the truth.

Eva looked away and gazed at the horizon where the sun was setting behind the picturesque rice paddocks. What a predicament she was in. Her only way to stop Damien Vanderbilt from becoming the president was to depend on China. If China's aid became public knowledge, Eva would destroy her chances of becoming the next US president. However, if Eva kept her association with China a secret, she would be no better than the candidates that she fought against. Eva decided to be honest to the American people, as the truth was more important than her ambitions.

Eva:

- I trust you, Eileen. But you should not have invited me to China. I do not intend to keep our association a secret.

Eileen:

- Admitting that China is helping you will destroy your aspirations of becoming the next US president.

Eva:

- That might be correct. What I do know is that I am not going to follow Damien's path of lying to the public to get elected. I want to make our association known. That is if you are willing to help me in my campaign.

Eileen:

- But wouldn't that breach the US laws against foreign interference?

Eva:

- I am sure that China had similar laws, yet here you are, being the president of a great nation.

Hearing this annoyed Eileen. She had never gotten over the fact that she became the president of China because of the same corporate enemies, which she had fought ever since. While she had won the election in 2023, history would never forget that Pierre Beaumont, Damien Vanderbilt, and Mitchell Cent made her the interim president of China in 2021, after the death of Jing Xi and the collapse of the Columnist Party. Eileen shook off her annoyance, stopping Damien and Pierre was more important than her ego.

Eileen:

- Very well. I am happy to announce China's support for you in the upcoming US election. I will assemble a press conference tomorrow evening. Until then, please examine these pieces of evidence about Reversogene.

Eva:

- Thank you, President Lu.

Eileen:

- You're welcome. I'll see you tomorrow.

Eva watched Eileen as she left the beautiful terrace as day turned into night. She felt excited to meet the inspirational Eileen Lu who had once been a prisoner of the genocidal tyrant Chairman Jing Xi. Rumours claimed that Eileen had killed Jing Xi when he tried to rape her, and Eva wanted these rumours to be true. Eileen's transformation from the rape victim of an evil dictator to the president of the world's largest democratic state served as an inspiration to Eva. Many hours later, Eva fell asleep after reading the evidence against Damien Vanderbilt throughout the night.

Chapter 10: Eva's Surge in the Polls terrify James Winter, 31st July 2028.

James Winter was drinking a glass of Macallan 25-Year-Old's 1962 Anniversary Malt whisky at the terrace of Palace Beaumont. Even though the whisky retailed at $10,000 a bottle, James could not enjoy the sumptuous taste. He needed to discuss some unwelcome news with Pierre, and he couldn't understand why the Swiss poof didn't take the issue seriously.

'Would you like some more ice for your Scotch, Mr Winter?', Pierre's assistant Jean asked. James lost his temper and yelled at her:

- No. I want you to fetch Pierre straight away. I have waited long enough.

Jean rushed off and James sighed. Although yelling at the servant hadn't helped, releasing his frustration was better than letting it boil over. James finished his expensive drink, and he looked at the blue lake from the hilltop palace. He turned around when he heard Pierre's annoying voice:

- Tsk, Tsk. Screaming at my servants won't help us against Eva Moreno.

James:

- If you were at home all this time, why did you make me wait for so long?

Pierre:

- For the same reason that you screamed at Jean. Because I can.

James:

- I don't have time for this. Eva Moreno is surging in the polls after exposing our and Damien's crimes.

Pierre:

- Who cares about polls? Ask Damien to release some fake polls. He controls 80 per cent of US media, so creating a narrative against Eva is a piece of cake. Particularly, since Eva admitted that China supports her.

James:

- Eva has exposed our crimes. This is going to have catastrophic consequences. Mitchell Cent suspended me as the CIA director when the news spread.

Pierre:

- Stop worrying. I will talk to Mitchell and I'll try to make him reinstate you. Otherwise, you can work for me. The main priority is to make Damien the next US president.

- As for me, the lawsuits that will follow Eva's announcement will bankrupt Reversogene Corporation. But I emptied that company of any money years ago, and the company has a figurehead CEO who will be my scapegoat.

James:

- At least look at the result of this polling.

Having said this, James transferred the polling data to Pierre's monocle and the results came up as a hologram in front of Pierre's vision. The following text accompanied the data: 'Predictive capability indicates a 72 % chance for Eva Moreno to win the election.'

Reading the monocle's prediction on the hologram vision unsettled Pierre. When the technology that helped him become the world's wealthiest man predicted that he would lose, he had reasons to worry.

Pierre sighed and replied:

- You might be onto something. We need to leverage our capabilities to discredit Eva. Her association with Eileen Lu and China should do the trick.

James:

- And what do you suggest that we do about the evidence against us?

Pierre shrugged his shoulders and replied:

- Who would dare to take us to court? Besides, with our control of the news and social media, people will focus on our enemies, while we can hide in the broad daylight.

- But to secure our future prosperity, we need Damien to win, and Mitchell Cent needs to protect us for the rest of his term.

James:

- Good. Will you visit Mitchell and ask for his support?

Pierre gave James a disdainful look. This was the best time of the year in Switzerland, and Pierre would not go back to America a few weeks after his last visit. Mitchell Cent would have to drag himself to Palace Beaumont to get his instructions. Pierre:

- I am not going back to America for a while. Mitchell will have to make his way here. Besides, do you want to go back to the USA where everyone knows you as the suspended CIA director?

James:

- How are you going to make Mitchell Cent come here on your whim?

Pierre:

- Tsk, tsk. Everyone knows that the President is a puppet. He will dance after my tune. Now I will retreat to my chambers. I suggest that you stay in one of the guestrooms in my palace, away from the prying eyes of the public.

James didn't reply. He had escaped the USA before some overzealous judge decided to put him on trial. James suspected that Pierre feared the same fate would befall him if he travelled to the USA. For now, James hoped that the president would sign an executive order that protected him.

Not wanting to bother Pierre further, James turned around, exited the room, and went to the guestroom that Jean had organised for him.

Chapter 11: Pierre Strikes a Deal with Mitchell Cent, 7th August 2028.

Pierre Beaumont was looking at the guests arriving at the reception area of Hotel d'Angleterre, located at Lake Geneva. To improve his reputation after the uncovering of the Reversogene scandal, Pierre had decided to lead a fundraiser as a distraction to the public. The objective of the fundraiser was to raise funds for poor villagers affected by a volcanic eruption in the Philippines. While Pierre didn't give a fuck about the poor villagers, Damien Vanderbilt, Pierre himself and James Winter needed to appear in a positive light.

Another important reason for the fundraiser was to entice the American puppet president Mitchell Cent to visit Pierre. Pierre didn't want some renegade judge in the USA to order his arrest, knowing the Reversogene scandal had been rampant over there, so he needed to secure Mitchell's support before setting foot in America.

Pierre saw Mitchell Cent entering the small and luxurious Parquet Louise conference room. Pierre decided to ignore him. While meeting with Mitchell Cent was crucial, Pierre didn't want others to realise this. Instead, he walked onto the stage. He set his monocle to give him a speech that "sway hearts" and gave a passionate speech about the importance of helping the survivors of natural disasters in South east Asia.

Once Pierre had finished with his speech, he got off the stage. As the camera crew left, Pierre smiled. Who would believe that he had deliberately released a dangerous medication via his pharmaceutical company Axil Azteca when he pledged billions of dollars to charity for the sake of humankind? The news corporation and social media that his peer Damien Vanderbilt controlled would label anyone speaking against him as a conspiracy theorist. This would deter most people from criticising Pierre and keep politicians obedient.

With the damage control done, Pierre went to his table to enjoy the dinner and the socialising with other banking executives. His conversation with Mitchell Cent would have to wait until later.

A FEW HOURS LATER, Pierre met with Mitchell Cent in a private meeting room at the hotel. Mitchell seemed a bit agitated and spoke:

- That was an impressive speech and display of charity from you, Pierre. Yet, I assume that it wasn't your true motivation for holding this fundraiser.

Pierre smirked:

- Public perception is everything. My emotional speech and my $2 billion donation to the survivors of the volcanic eruption will sway the masses in my favour. Who will believe that I've made my fortune from deliberately releasing the Hei Bai virus and the unreliable Reversogene cure of the virus itself? That would be preposterous!

Mitchell:

- I haven't heard any allegations about your releasing the virus. The consensus is that Chairman Jing Xi was the one that released it as a biological attack on us.

Pierre looked away for a second, and he bit his tongue. Why had he suggested that he might be behind the Hei Bai virus outbreak? There was no point in dwelling on it, so Pierre replied:

- You're correct. I read too much of what people say about me on the Internet. A bad habit of mine.

Mitchell laughed:

- You wouldn't last a day as the President of the USA if you cared about political rants online.

- So, how can I help you and the World Bank?

Pierre:

- I need you to sign an executive order that grants me, James Winter, and Damien Vanderbilt diplomatic immunity for the rest of your term.

Mitchell:

- Diplomatic immunity? I don't understand. James and Damien are American citizens and you are a not a diplomat.

Pierre:

- We are global citizens and spokespeople for a global movement. As such, we should have the same degree of protection as other diplomats.

Mitchell:

- I doubt people will appreciate if I grant you immunity, Pierre.

Pierre:

- Bah. You said that you don't care about political criticism. Besides, you are 69-years old and retiring this year. Why not live out the rest of your life in wealth and affluence. Money is, as you know, not a problem.

Mitchell shook his head and replied:

- I don't need your money. Too much wealth would only alienate me from God.

Pierre took a deep breath. He hadn't anticipated Mitchell refusing his bribe. Then again, everyone had a price, Pierre needed to find out what Mitchell desired. Could God be the answer? Pierre decided to give it a shot.

Pierre:

- My wealth can help you spread your religious doctrine. What better way to spend your retirement than preaching the true word of God?

Mitchell:

- You have a point. If protecting you and Damien can save countless souls, so be it. I need to spread the true words of Jesus Christ, for the sake of humanity.

Pierre:

- Excellent. We know that you are currently writing your own memoirs into a book. If you sign the executive order protecting us, one of Damien's publishing houses will offer you $10 million for your memoirs. In the book, you can share your views on the truth about your much-loved Jesus Christ.

Mitchell:

- We have a deal. I know that you are not a god-fearing person, but thanks for helping me spread God's words.

- I need to return to my room. As the president of the USA, I have a busy schedule tomorrow.

Pierre nodded and replied:

- Thank you. May God bless you.

As Mitchell left, Pierre sighed of relief. For a brief moment, Pierre had feared that Mitchell was incorruptible. As it turned out, Mitchell just needed another form of motivation. Pierre hoped that Damien would be willing to publish Mitchell's memoirs as it would be annoying to acquire a publishing company and do it himself. Pierre got into his limousine and went back to Palace Beaumont. He felt satisfied that the issues with Eva Moreno and Reversogene drug would soon be under control.

AS PIERRE ENTERED PALACE Beaumont, he noticed an unexpected visitor. Sandra Santiago, the adoptive daughter of his Brazilian business partner Josefina Fiero, walked up to Pierre and hugged him:

- Pierre, it's so nice to see you again.

Pierre didn't reciprocate Sandra's hug and instead he whinged:

- Stop this charade, Sandra.
- Tell me why you are here?

Sandra stopped hugging Pierre and took a step back. She smirked:

- I am turning 18 in a couple of months, so Josefina wanted me to learn how to become wealthy and influential.

Pierre shook his head. While he was certain that the young and beautiful Sandra would be a suitable partner if he wanted an heir, he had already organised that several years earlier. Pierre had paid a multitude of surrogate mothers to bear and raise his children, having lived an unmarried life for the past 58 years. This way, he could pick the most suitable successor when he approached the end of his days. As for Sandra's youth and beauty, Pierre couldn't care less. He liked mature men, not young girls.

Pierre taunted:

- I am afraid Josefina hasn't done her research. I prefer mature men over young women. Thus, while I am sure many men would find you seductive, I find your advances irritating.

- Now tell me what you want.

Sandra sighed and replied:

- Josefina wants to summon everyone in the Monocle Conspiracy to Brazil. She has heard about your aspiration to make Damien Vanderbilt the president of the USA. She is willing to help, for a price.

Pierre laughed:

- It is always about money, isn't it?

- Sending me an email would be easier than sending you to seduce me. Nonetheless, let me show you to a room. It is past midnight and it is too late to discuss business.

Sandra nodded and Pierre showed Sandra to a guestroom on the third floor. As Pierre walked back to his bedroom, he reflected over Sandra's beauty. She was extraordinary and if he hadn't been aligned the other way, she could have seduced him and exerted power over him. In the end, it didn't matter. Josefina's powerplay had failed, but he would play along, and he would give her the money it took to make her cooperative. Money was, after all, not a problem.

Chapter 12: The Monocle Conspiracy Meets in Brazil, 12th August 2028.

Josefina Fiero watched how one of her servants carried in a tray of cocktails. It was the dry season and the sun was shining; thus, it was the perfect conditions to assemble her associates. Josefina looked at the rare birds she had assembled in the large private park surrounding her palace. In this serene environment, she could forget about the turmoil that was affecting the rest of her home country.

Josefina's private palace was a replica of the white house and it was an extension of Josefina's ego. Although she would never rule over the actual white house, presiding in her replica was even better. Besides, she was more powerful than the American president. At least she had felt that way until her failed attempt at interfering in the Brazilian election the previous year. Since her chosen candidate had failed, the Brazilian president had disrupted Josefina's business with frivolous lawsuits. While Josefina felt certain that she could win in court, she wanted to make sure that she would win. Securing the support of Pierre Beaumont, the richest man in the world, was her best bet.

Josefina thought about the upcoming meeting. She hoped Vladimir Kravchenko would not attend. While Vladimir's murder of Jorge Santiago had played out in Josefina's favour, she knew that his presence would upset Sandra. Because of the murder, Josefina had been able to adopt Sandra, who filled her with pride, and would be the successor to Josefina's business empire.

While Josefina had upheld contact with the other members of the Monocle Conspiracy, this was the first time they assembled in over two years. During their last meeting, they had tried to uncover an alien artefact in Colombia. That mission had been a failure, and they had been seconds from dying when sentry robots had attacked them. They had survived the ordeal, however, and Josefina knew that she could never achieve her goals if she was too risk-averse.

A servant approached Josefina and spoke:

- A senhora Josefina. Elaine Orchard, do Conglomerado Harapan, está aqui. *(Ms. Josefina, Elaine Orchard from the Harapan Conglomerate is here.)*

Josefina:

- Obrigado, Evelina. Vou ótimo aqui na sala de coquetéis. *(Thank you, Evelina. Bring them to the cocktail room.)*

JOSEFINA APPROACHED Elaine Orchard, who was sipping on a cool Caipirinha. Elaine looked younger and fresher than ever and seeing this filled the slightly older Josefina with jealousy. When they first met in Nepal eight years earlier, Josefina had still maintained the stunning looks from her youth. But now when they were both in their mid-40s, Josefina's looks had faded while Elaine still looked fresher than ever. Josefina decided to fake it, as she needed to speak to Elaine in confidence before the meeting. Josefina:

- Oh my god. Elaine, you look amazing! What is your secret?

Elaine smiled and replied:

- I found the fountain of youth and my scientists at The Harapan Conglomerate managed to replicate the formula. This facial treatment will make you look a decade younger.

Having said this, Elaine passed a jar of Kalaotoa Island mud to Josefina, who smiled and replied:

- Thank you very much. I can't wait to try it.

Josefina put the jar aside, picked up a drink from a tray and cheered:

- Cheers to us. Together we will shape our continents to the better.

Elaine:

- Yes, indeed. The first step of our plan is working out. I allowed Eileen Lu's spy to steal the evidence against Pierre, to force him to finance our plans. With the world's richest man bankrolling us, nothing can stop our long-term plans.

Josefina:

- Yes. For too long the bankers have robbed our nations and made us weak. Now we can make our nations great while weakening our rivals.

Elaine:

- Yes. So, what is your opinion about Eva Moreno? Should we support her or Damien Vanderbilt?

Josefina:

- We should support Damien. Josefina would be a good president for the USA. She would crush Pierre and rebuild her country. But we are better off if the USA has a corrupt president that makes them weak while we siphon money from the World Bank. That's how we become stronger.

Elaine:

- So, are you saying that we should support Damien, knowing that he will destroy America?

Josefina:

- Yes. I hope that doesn't bother you?

Elaine took a sip of the Caipirinha and smirked:

- It doesn't bother me at all. Oh, and I love this drink.

Josefina:

- I am happy to hear that. Let's enjoy a few more and coordinate our business plans. We have so much to catch up on.

Having said this, Josefina rang a bell and ordered some more drinks. After that, Elaine and Josefina got drunk, socialised, and coordinated their business plans for the rest of the evening.

THE FOLLOWING DAY, Josefina's head felt like someone had punched her with a sledgehammer. She had enjoyed far too many drinks the night before. A meeting with Elaine was a rare opportunity for Josefina to socialise with some-one with similar ambitions. Having a Zetan Monocle was both a blessing and a curse, as it altered the mind and made it harder to socialise with other humans. Since Elaine was in the same situation, they had drunk and gossiped late into the night. This was something that Pierre's whiny voice had some objections to.
Pierre:

- I am disappointed with you, Josefina. I had anticipated a proper re-ception when I arrived last night. Instead, I found the two of you blind drunk and gossiping.

Josefina didn't respond. She had drunk too much, and Pierre was too im-portant to disregard. She lined up some cocaine and snorted it. As the effect kicked in, she felt better. Josefina:

- Relax with the attitude, Pierre. You are not the centre of the uni-verse. Besides, we are here to discuss how to make your candidate, Damien Vanderbilt win the US election.

Pierre scoffed:

- Bah, I would prefer a hostess that didn't cure her hangover with co-caine.

Ben Yehuda intervened:

- Cut the crap, Pierre. My brother and I haven't travelled all the way here to listen to your bickering. Let's get back on topic.

Pierre nodded at Ben Yehuda. Ben and Szymon Yehuda were two Israeli brothers who had been on the same trip as Pierre when they found the Zetan Monocles in Nepal. Pierre had funded their mission to find the primordial Zeto Crystal, but it had been to no avail so far. Despite this, it was important to keep them on the payroll. Through James Winter and the Yehuda Brothers, Pierre controlled the Mossad and the CIA. Through this partnership, he had something that was even more important than money, which was information. Pierre sighed:

- You're correct, Ben. My apologies for wasting your time. Let's focus on the issue at hand.

Szymon:

- Not so fast, Pierre. We need to know where Martin and Vladimir are.

Pierre sighed and replied:

- Vladimir is in a coma after a botched mission. Martin is a broken man who has withdrawn to a secluded island in the Pacific.

Sandra taunted:

- Such a shame with Vladimir. Can I pull the plug on that bastard?

Pierre gave Sandra an angry look and replied:

- No, you cannot. Vladimir is an essential member of my inner circle and he has been crucial in aiding our cause.

Sandra:

- Whatever you say, Pierre.

Josefina brought the conversation back on track:

- So, how would it benefit the rest of us if Damien Vanderbilt wins the Presidential election?

Pierre:

- Well for starters, it keeps me out of prison so I can keep funding your operations. Besides, with Damien as the US president, all of you will receive lucrative US government contracts.

Josefina:

- That's all good, but I need something concrete. We have expenses, after all.

Pierre:

- Very well. If you choose to help me, I will give you $1 billion each. That should be enough to cover your conflict with the Brazilian president, Josefina. It will also be enough to fund the Templar order and our continued search for the Zeto crystals, Ben and Szymon.

Josefina:

- That should be acceptable. What do you need from us?

Pierre:

- For now, I need you to use your influence to support Damien and discredit Eva Moreno and Barry O'Connor in international media. I might need you to perform covert operations as well, but my generous donations will cover your expenses.

Josefina smiled at Pierre and replied:

- I agree to your terms, Pierre. What about the rest of you?

Ben Yehuda:

- We agree to this arrangement.

Elaine:

- I am also happy with this arrangement.

Josefina:

- That's excellent news. Let's enjoy some Churrasco. I have ordered my chefs to make it Kosher, to honour our Israeli guests.

After saying this, Josefina rang a bell to alert her employees. Chefs entered the room, carrying big platters with assorted grilled meats and side dishes. As the group feasted on the meats, and drank expensive wines, they made detailed plans for the months to come.

Chapter 13: Pierre and James travel to China to pressure Eileen Lu, 2nd September 2028.

Pierre Beaumont and James Winter were sitting on a private jet headed for China. Developments had been unsatisfying, and Eva Moreno had a large lead in the polls despite Pierre's and Damien's attempts at discrediting her. Due to the political situation, President Mitchell Cent hadn't dared to reinstate James Winter as the CIA director. This meant Pierre did not have access to CIA data, which was not ideal for his plans. With this in mind, Pierre had taken a gamble to travel to China and confront Eileen Lu. If China withdrew their financial support to Eva, her candidacy would drown in the media cacophony that Pierre and Damien organised against her.

Jean walked up to Pierre and topped up his glass with red wine. As she left, James complained:

- You shouldn't drink that much wine. We need to focus on our meeting with Eileen.

Pierre:

- Don't talk to me like that. I am a connoisseur and I can handle my drink.

James:

- Fucking hell, Pierre. We should discuss our plans. Instead, you're drinking and ignoring me. We are equals.

Pierre taunted:

- We are not equals.

- I am the world's wealthiest man, and you are a disgraced government employee who has been hiding in my palace. Now sit back and enjoy your wine in silence. Domaine Leroy Chambertin Grand Cru 1990 is too expensive to be left to go to waste.

James:

- I don't care about wines anymore. All I want is to get back to Melinda and her children.

Pierre:

- Bah. Trading a glamorous life of wine and women to raise someone else's progeny. Pathetic.

James:

- Look who is talking. You have a lot of children, Pierre.

Pierre:

- Yes, a dozen children with a dozen surrogate mothers. Six boys and six girls. All turning 4 this year. As a prominent man, my dream is to have a diverse pool of progeny so I can choose a suitable successor when the time comes. That doesn't mean I like children.

James:

- I could tell when I attended your quarterly inspection last week. You showed a chilling level of contempt for your children when you met them.

Pierre:

- Yes. I must admit my disappointment with the 2024 batch of surrogacy. Hopefully, I can master genetic modification and produce a better batch in the future. Genetics is an interesting topic, and we can only learn from our mistakes.

Having said this, Pierre recalled the latest quarterly inspection of his progeny. Back in 2023, Pierre had paid a dozen women to mother his children. Once the children were born, he had opened a centre where his employees worked to raise the children according to Pierre's desired specifications. The program had been an abject failure this far, and the only children with actual potential were the twins Lucien and Delphine. Pierre had thought of ending the program and culling the children, but he had stopped. The risk of detection was too high, and Pierre didn't want infanticide to be his downfall. Pierre spoke again:

- Thinking back to the inspection, Lucien and Delphine showed some potential. No matter, I have many years left, and I will revisit the program at a later stage.

James:

- You're a very sick and demented man, Pierre.

Pierre:

- Bah, there is a fine line between insanity and genius. Now shut up and enjoy your wine.

James did as Pierre instructed. After sculling his wine, he put on a blindfold and he fell asleep.

PIERRE BEAUMONT WAS tapping the glass table irritably, waiting for Eileen Lu to receive him. Pierre hated when people made him wait, as it was beneath him waiting for others. Yet, there was nothing he could do to make her hurry up. Pierre regretted that he had fast-tracked Eileen to become the president of China after the collapse of Chairman Jing Xi's Columnist Party. For seven long years, Pierre had suffered Eileen's ingratitude, and this was the last straw. By exposing Pierre's crimes and supporting Eva Moreno, Eileen had declared war on the man who made her.

Eileen Lu entered the meeting room, accompanied by a large group of bodyguards. As Eileen shook Pierre's hand, Pierre complained:

- I asked for a private meeting. Not to meet you and half of China's army!

Eileen shrugged her shoulders and replied:

- I have seen the capabilities that your monocles give a trained warrior. I assume that former CIA director James Winter is an accomplished warrior like the late Vladimir Kravchenko. Why else would you bring him here?

Pierre:

- Bah, Vladimir is not dead, and I wouldn't come here to kill you myself.

Eileen gave Pierre a cold stare. Pierre backed down and replied:

- Very well. We'll take off our monocles.

Having said this, Pierre nodded to James and they took off their monocles and put them in the inner pockets of their suits. When they removed the monocles, they revealed their purple predatory eyes on the righthand side of their faces.

Eileen:

- What did you do to your eyes?

Pierre stated:

- Our monocles' connection to the optical nerve changes the colour of the iris. It's a nuisance but in the grand scheme of things, it's insignificant.

Eileen:

- Where did you get those things from? I remember Vladimir wore one of them when he saved me from the wrath of Jing Xi. He shot down two pursuing fighter jets with a rifle during our escape.

Pierre joked dryly:

- Yes, he always spoke about that episode. It was the highlight of his illustrious career.

- Anyway, now that we have taken off our monocles, would you mind a private meeting?

Eileen shook her head and gestured towards most of her guards to leave the room. Pierre:

- Thank you, Eileen.

Eileen:

- Now tell me why you are here?

Pierre:

- Because you need to stop supporting Eva Moreno in her bid to become the US president.

Eileen:

- I won't withdraw my support from Eva. I have met her, and our values align. Eva would be a good leader for her nation and good for the world. She is the opposite of your candidate, Damien Vanderbilt, who only seek to enrichen himself and his accomplices.

Pierre:

- This is unacceptable. I saved you and I made you who you are. You should obey me.

Eileen:

- I am not your puppet president, Pierre. If there is nothing else, please leave my office.

Pierre knew that he was better off not taunting the Chinese Dragon, but he couldn't control himself.
He yelled with his shrill voice:

- You must obey me, Eileen, or I will destroy China's economy.

Eileen:

- That's enough, Pierre. From this day on, I expel you and James Winter from China. You will not be allowed to return. Guards, escort our guests to the airport.

James Winter intervened and pulled Pierre away. Threatening Eileen Lu while they were in China was unwise and they were lucky that Eileen Lu was not a blood-thirsty tyrant like her predecessor. *Shut up and comply,* James whispered in Pierre's ear. Pierre calmed down and Chinese soldiers escorted them back to their private jet at the airport.

JAMES AND PIERRE WERE back on the private jet when James shouted:

- What the hell is wrong with you? You almost got us killed.

Pierre:

- I was testing her. I suspected that she was a weak bleeding heart and this proves it. While we couldn't persuade her to stop support-ing Eva, we can destroy her economy and force her out of the race.

James:

- And what if she had decided to kill us in her office?

Pierre:

- She wouldn't. If she had wanted me dead, she would have wanted a public trial. That would be disastrous for her.

James sighed. There was no point in arguing with Pierre, who believed in his superior intellect and would never admit any wrongdoing.
James:

- So, what are we doing now?

Pierre:

- I will make good of my threat. Eileen Lu and China will suffer as I will direct the World Bank's power of the international banking systems against China and use Damien's news and social media influence against her. I will stop all overseas banking transactions to and from China, bringing Eileen to the brink of ruin. This will force her to cooperate.

- Now please refrain from talking. I have plenty of important dignitaries to contact!

Having said this, Pierre inserted his monocle and he started contacting all the global banking dignitaries. It was time for Eileen Lu to experience the full extent of his power.

Chapter 14: Damien Vanderbilt visits Pierre Beaumont, 8th September 2028.

Pierre sighed as he closed the email from the Deutsche Bank chairman, Gunter Fritz. Another major banker had refused to help him in his economic crusade against China. This was not how Pierre had intended things to go. He needed compliance among the other bankers in his economic war against China. Otherwise, he would lose this war and China would be able to participate in the global economy. Jean entered Pierre's home office and spoke:

- Monsieur Beaumont. Damien Vanderbilt is here.

Pierre sighed. Why on Earth did people arrive at his mansion unannounced all the time? In the last few months, James Winter, Sandra Santiago, and now Damien Vanderbilt had arrived without prior notification. Pierre hoped that Damien would follow Sandra's example and go home after the meeting, as James Winter seemed to be impossible to get rid of. That uncultured Yankee had occupied one of the Palace Beaumont guestrooms for the last six weeks. Pierre:

- Well, it would be rude to keep him waiting. Bring Damien some refreshments. I will meet him in the dining room.

Jean nodded and left the room. Pierre got up and made his way to his bedroom where he got dressed in a tuxedo with the Beaumont family crest. He rarely wore clothes with the crest, but the attire was suitable for a meeting with the next American president.

Pierre studied himself in the mirror while he wore the tuxedo. He felt proud donning the family crest while being the epitome of success. Being the sole survivor of the family's line, Pierre had gotten expelled from Palace Beaumont as a young boy, growing up amongst foster parents. But he had worked himself to a position of considerable wealth and power and bought back the palace. Pierre's wealth and power had been amplified when he found the Zetan Monocle in 2020 and when he released the Hei Bai virus a year later. Since then, Pierre had been the wealthiest and most influential man in the world. Thanks to his breeding program, he would have enough progeny to create a dynasty that would rule the world. Pierre smiled; it was time to meet the next puppet president of the USA.

DAMIEN VANDERBILT WAS tapping on his smartphone when Pierre entered the dining room. Pierre gave Damien a quick look before speaking. Damien looked tired and his clothes, although expensive, looked unkempt and wrinkly.

Pierre cleared his throat and spoke:

- Welcome to Palace Beaumont. Apologies for the lack of entertainment. I never received your meeting request.

Damien:

- I never sent one. I have a very busy schedule with my election campaign.

Pierre:

- Bah, if you can't handle a campaign, follow Joe Bitten's strategy from 2020 and campaign from your basement, blaming the coronavirus pandemic.

Damien shook his head and replied:

- I am not elderly so I can't cite "avoiding the flu" as a valid reason to not campaign in person. Besides, Joe Bitten lost to that fuckwit Deidrick Dump, so it didn't work out for him.

Pierre smirked:

  - He didn't miss out on much. He died from dementia the following year.

Damien:

  - And Deidrick died from contracting the Hei Bai virus. Funny how things work out.

Pierre:

  - Yes. But Mitchell Cent has served us well. Hiding behind a cloak of zeal, he has made sure to fulfil all our needs.

Damien:

  - But he cannot protect us if Eva wins the election. If I don't win, we are toast.

Pierre:

  - Agreed. Eva winning the election would be an unacceptable outcome.

Damien:

  - So, why haven't you acted against Eileen Lu? You promised that you'd make her stop supporting Eva Moreno when I spoke to you last week.

Pierre sighed, walked over to his whiskey collection, and poured himself a drink. He hated admitting that his plan had faced a hiccup, but the truth was that he needed the other major bankers to wage economic warfare against China. Pierre:

  - There has been a complication. My colleagues believe economic warfare against China will harm their interests.

Damien:

- That's ridiculous. When I become the president, I can make the Federal Reserve print trillions of dollars to finance their expenses.

Pierre:

- Yes, but money printing can't go on forever. My colleagues at World Bank federation need real assets and potential benefits to support you against Eva Moreno and her Chinese alliance.

Damien:

- What other assets do you have in mind?

Pierre:

- There are still large areas in the USA that are kept preserved as wildlife national parks. If you promise to cancel these land protections and transfer the land ownerships to private interests, I am sure we can reach an agreement.

Damien hesitated. Even though he was a dishonest man that spread lies and propagandas through his news and social media network, he still appreciated the beauty of nature. Besides, countries without environmental protections ended up facing wanton ecological and economic disaster. Damien shook his head and replied:

- I cannot agree to those terms.

Pierre taunted:

- What a shame. I am sure Eva would love to beat you in the election and throw you into prison.

Damien:

- No, she won't. We will convince her to pull out of the election.

Pierre:

- We? How are we going to do that?

Damien:

- Yes, you are coming with me. You have as much to lose from Eva becoming the president as I have. Even more if she finds proof that you were behind the Hei Bai Virus outbreak. If that's the case, there will be nowhere for you to run, Pierre.

Hearing Damien's statement filled Pierre with fear, and he struggled to contain his act of arrogance. He walked to the bar, poured himself some more scotch, and sculled it. Pierre:

- Very well. I am coming with you. Let's meet with this Eva Moreno.

Damien:

- My car is waiting outside, we are leaving at once.

Pierre nodded and replied:

- Understood. I'll go upstairs and fetch James Winter. We'll need his expertise and connections to stop Eva.

After saying this, Pierre went upstairs to fetch James. A short while later, the three of them walked to Damien's limousine for a transfer to the airport.

While they were in the car, Pierre sat in silence and thought carefully. Although he hated that Damien had arrived at his house and given him orders, he had to comply. Damien hinting that he knew about Pierre's involvement in the Hei Bai Virus outbreak meant that Pierre had to obey Damien. If the truth came out about Reversogene and the Hei Bai Virus outbreak, nothing could save Pierre from being sentenced to a lifetime in prison!

Chapter 15: Pierre and James try to influence Eva Moreno, 10ᵗʰ September 2028.

Pierre Beaumont exited his private jet at the small regional airport in Santa Fe, the capital of New Mexico. Despite the summer being over, it was still a sizzling hot day in this southern state of the USA. Eva Moreno had refused to meet them, but Pierre would not take no for an answer. He would sneak in and speak to her after her campaign meeting. He turned to James Winter and spoke:

- Are you ready to confront Eva?

James:

- I am not keen to assassinate Eva. There are cameras everywhere, and we better send someone else while we have an alibi.

Pierre:

- Tsk, Tsk. We are not going to murder Eva at this stage. Let's first investigate whether we can come to an agreement with her. Perhaps, a hefty sum for her retirement fund or a position in Damien's cabinet will win her over.

James:

- I don't think so. Her refusal to meet with you should be indicative to her predisposition.

Pierre:

- You might be right. No matter, I'd rather find a peaceful solution than resorting to violence. If we have Eva murdered, her voters might swing to the senile Barry O'Connor from the Democrat Party. It is better to win her over. That way, Damien will win the election, while we maintain the status quo at a minimal expense.

James:

- Very well. Let's head to the convention centre. Eva will speak soon.

PIERRE WAS STANDING on the street watching the crowds cheering Eva's speech. He hoped Eva had paid the crowds to be her audience, because if all these people had come by their own free will, it would be hard for Damien Vanderbilt to beat Eva Moreno. Damien always had huge crowds, but he paid most of them to attend. This was an embarrassing fact that they worked hard to cover up.

Pierre queried his monocle of the best way to confront Eva and it showed 'Pretend to be catering staff.' He turned to James and spoke:

- Does your monocle also tell you to pretend to be a bloody waiter?

James:

- Yes.

- Those men over there look like catering staff and they have convention centre uniforms. Let's have a chat with them.

Pierre was disappointed. This was the reason that he preferred to send Vladimir on missions. Having to pretend to be a servant to meet a politician was below him, but it was crucial to the plan. James led the way, took out a bundle of $100 bills and they approached the waiters. James:

- Hey guys, how does five hundred dollars for not going to work sound?

Waiter:

- Sounds like the best plan ever.

James smiled and handed the money to the waiters. He spoke:

- The money is yours if you give me your uniform shirt and your passkey, and head home.

The waiters hesitated for a while, but they gave in to the temptation and shortly afterwards Pierre and James were waiting in Eva's greenroom.

EVA MORENO STARED IN shock when she entered her greenroom and she saw James Winter and Pierre Beaumont. Pierre spoke:

- Eva Moreno, we meet at last.

Eva:

- Why are you here? I told you that I did not want to meet you.

Pierre:

- If you had agreed to meet me, I would not come here dressed as a waiter.

Eva took up a two-way radio and was about to summon security when Pierre interrupted her:

- Please, Eva. Hear me out, it will be worthwhile.

Eva put down her radio, gave Pierre a cold stare, and replied:

- Okay. I'll give you one minute to state your business.

Pierre:

- Eva, even if you win the presidency, it will be for nothing. The Democrats and the Republicans will never accept an independent candidate, neither will the judges in the Supreme Court. You'll be stuck in limbo for four years and people will remember you as a failure.

Eva:

- I am aware of the difficulties, but I don't understand why you made all this effort to taunt me?

Pierre:

- Because I am offering you an alternative. Withdraw your candidacy and pledge your support to Damien Vanderbilt. Once he wins the election, he'll make you the minister for whatever department you want to be in. You'll have real power to change the world and you'll be financially secure for life.

Hearing this, Eva picked up the radio and called security:

- Eva Moreno to security, I have two intruders in my greenroom. Please remove them.

Eva put down the radio and spoke to Pierre:

- I would never sell out my integrity like this. You are going to prison, Pierre.

Pierre was about to say something, but security guards stormed in and expelled them. After that, the guards handed them over to the cops who drove them off to police custody.

Chapter 16: Pierre and Damien convince the Global Banking Cabal to engage in economic warfare against China, 17th September 2028.

Pierre was feeling uncomfortable in a cheap and ill-fitting waiter uniform. The idiots at the Santa Fe police department had 'misplaced' his property and he had lost his tailor-made suits and Swiss watches. The four days that Pierre had spent in jail meant that he didn't have time to go home and get his tailor-made outfits pressed and cleaned.

Pierre sighed. It had been embarrassing to spend four days with low-class criminals in jail. Mitchell Cent had certainly taken his time to pardon Pierre's intrusion at the convention centre.

Pierre entered the boardroom where he intended to gather the leaders of the major banking conglomerates in the world. The men in the room controlled 90 % of all overseas transactions, which would be enough to bring China and her president Eileen Lu to her knees.

Damien caught a glimpse of Pierre. He put down the cup of coffee he was drinking, and he taunted:

- Hello Pierre. How was jail? Was it like Four Seasons or like Swisso-tel?

Pierre frowned and replied:

- I would have preferred if Mitchell Cent had hurried up. I spent four days living and eating with peasants. Such a disaster!

Damien laughed and replied:

- I don't understand why you broke into Eva's greenroom with James? Did you lose your mind?

Pierre:

- Eva impressed me. She would have been invaluable if I could turn her to our cause.

Damien:

- That will never happen.

Pierre:

- That is correct. That's why we need to make sure that Eva will never use her talents as the next US president. To achieve that end, do you agree to revoke environmental protections and give up governmental ownership of the wildlife national parks in favour of the support from my fellow bankers?

Damien:

- I will do whatever it takes to win this election. If I need to give up our national parks to knock Eva Moreno and her Chinese alliance out of the race, so be it.

Pierre:

- Excellent. I will speak to the others and I am sure that we'll come to an agreement.

Having said this, Pierre rang a bell and a waiter entered the room. A short while later, Pierre was enjoying a peppermint tea while waiting for the other dignitaries.

PIERRE WATCHED IN CONTEMPT as the sweaty, obese, and caviar-smelling Gunter Fritz, the head of the Deutsche Bank, entered the boardroom. Gunter was from the northern German-speaking parts of Switzerland and there was no racial group that Pierre had more disdain for. How could anyone speak such an uncultured barbaric language when they lived in a country where French was also an official language?

Gunter and Pierre were the same age, and they had been rivals since they were both entry-level bankers at Deutsche Bank, 35 years earlier. Born into an ailing noble family, Pierre felt contempt for the lower classes, and it had destroyed him when Gunter got promoted instead of him. Pierre had left Deutsche Bank to work for the World Bank, and the rest was history. Pierre was now the wealthiest man on the planet and had numerous world-class international bankers under his grip.

Gunter got seated, turned to Pierre, and spoke:

- Pierre, I hope that you have secured the deal that you promised us. I would hate to travel all the way to New York to listen to more vague promises.

Pierre:

- I have discussed the matter with Damien. If he becomes the next President, he will repeal the protection of the wildlife national parks. He will grant you the mining rights at Yellowstone National Park. The area is rich in rare earth minerals due to the vicinity to the volcano.

Gunter:

- That is not enough. I need the US government to guarantee all my future investments. My mines will be worthless if the volcano erupts.

Pierre:

- That shouldn't be a problem. The Federal Reserve can guarantee them by printing more money and provide you with investment funding.

Gunter:

- I don't want money. The way the Federal Reserve is printing money, the US dollar will soon have the same value as toilet paper. I want gold!

Pierre glanced at the Federal Reserve Chairman, Angus Brothschild, who shook his head. Pierre sighed; he would have to put his own gold on the line if he wanted a deal. Pierre:

- I will guarantee the gold from my personal reserves. How much gold do you need as a guarantee for your Yellowstone National Park investment?

Gunter smirked and licked his lips:

- 10,000 metric tonnes of gold will suffice.

Pierre stared at Gunter in disbelief. 10,000 metric tonnes of gold were 5 percent of all gold on the planet. All of this to guarantee the investment on one mining complex. "That bloody volcano better not erupt." Pierre muttered to himself. He turned to Gunter and spoke:

- I agree to your terms. I will guarantee your mining project at Yellowstone once your contribution has led to Damien becoming the president of the USA.

Gunter grinned slyly:

- Then we have an agreement, Pierre. I am sure that my fellow banker are looking for similar guarantees from you and the World Bank.

Pierre sighed. He knew that the others had ganged up on him and this would ruin him. However, he had to agree for now, but he would word the agreements so he would never have to pay.

A gruelling half an hour later, Pierre had agreed to guarantee the others with 50,000 metric tonnes of gold. Purchasing these amounts would drive up the gold price to astronomical levels, but he would find a way and the others would suffer for ganging up on him. For now, all that mattered was to crush Eva Moreno and drive her out of the American election, and to not let the truth of the origin of the Hei Bai virus outbreaks be known.

Chapter 17: Eileen Lu gives in to Pierre's demands, 4th October 2028.

Pierre was sitting in front of his fireplace in Palace Beaumont. He was in a great mood. The goose liver, the beluga caviar and the vintage wine tasted better than ever, and Pierre had turned the previous month's defeat into a great win.

Realising that he needed to acquire 50,000 tonnes of gold to guarantee the other world bankers' investments had terrified Pierre. But he had found a way to turn his predicament into success. Pierre had used Damien's media influence to spread fake stories about the discovery of abundant goldfields on earth, rendering gold worthless. The alleged discovery of huge quantities of gold had caused retail investors to panic-sell their gold at low prices. Thus, through creating a false narrative through Damien's social media and news networks, Pierre had turned his predicament into an opportunity to amass gold at a very low cost. The value of gold would skyrocket back to its normal high when people found out that the discovery of the massive amounts of gold were a hoax.

Pierre put down his wineglass, picked up a gold bar, and stroke it. What an amazing feeling it was to touch something so beautiful and priceless at the same time. Jean Valmont entered Pierre's lounge room and interrupted his passionate moment with the gold bar. Jean:

- Monsieur Pierre. Eileen Lu and a delegation from China have arrived.

Pierre smirked:

- How lovely! Please tell them to go to the Grand Dining Hall. My chefs have cooked a meal worthy of this occasion. I will see them after dinner.

Jean nodded and left the room.

Pierre clutched the gold bar to his chest, and he stroke it like a baby. This was his moment of glee. Eileen Lu had come to surrender in the economic war that she started by refusing to submit to his authority. It was poetic justice that the woman he had elevated to power, had come to admit his dominance.

EILEEN LU WAS EATING a beef eye fillet with potato gratin when Pierre entered the dining room. Pierre:

> - How was the steak? Such a shame you couldn't wait for me to arrive. Such uncultured behaviour.

Eileen:

> - Your employee told us that you would arrive after dinner.

Pierre:

> - Oh, did she? Tsk, tsk. I guess you don't understand Swiss etiquette. Regardless of what my servant tells you, you are meant to wait for the master of the household before dining.

> - No matter, we have a more important topic to discuss.

Eileen sighed. She regretted that she hadn't imprisoned Pierre when he had pressed her in China. If she did, this situation wouldn't have come to pass. Then again, if she allowed herself to be a tyrant that imprisoned and murdered people on a whim, she wouldn't be the leader that she aspired to be. Eileen spoke:

> - Your unlawful economic warfare against my nation is causing great suffering among my people. Now all international bankers have put sanctions against Chinese financial transactions. It needs to end.

Pierre smirked:

- I am willing to discuss the sanctions the international banking community applied to China for influencing the American election. All you need to do is to stop supporting Eva Moreno. Political leaders should not interfere in foreign elections.

Eileen:

- Hold on. You lobbied to change the US law, so you were able to influence the 2024 re-election of Mitchell Cent. What is the difference?

Pierre:

- The difference is that I am not a politician and I don't represent a nation.

- I assume that you are here to achieve results and not to discuss philosophy. Stop supporting Eva Moreno, and I will discuss ending international banking restrictions against China with my peers.

Eileen:

- So, will the sanctions end if I stop supporting Eva Moreno?

Pierre:

- Doing so would increase the possibility of a favourable outcome. The Chinese elections are coming up in January. You should focus on your own election.

Eileen sighed. She looked at Pierre's face and tried to understand his intentions, but she was empty-handed. Supporting Eva came at an excessive cost for herself and her people. Pierre and the international banks were powerful foes, and this conflict could tank the Chinese economy. If the economy failed, her re-election hopes would come to naught. Eileen:

- Okay, I'll withdraw my support for Eva Moreno.

Pierre:

- Good. When I receive proof that you are fulfilling your promises, my colleagues and I will discuss the cessation of our sanctions against your nation.

- Now please leave. Your presence is as unwanted in Palace Beaumont, as mine is in China. Au revoir, Eileen.

Eileen got up and commanded her delegation:

- Gāi zǒule. Ràng wǒmen bùyào yúyuè wǒmen de huānyíng. *(Let's go now. Do not let these people treat us with disrespect.)*

After hearing this, everyone in Eileen's delegation left without a word.

PIERRE WAS ENJOYING a glass of smoky whisky, while dressed up in a World War 2 uniform owned by his grandfather Vincent Beaumont. He looked at the portrait of his late grandfather and spoke:

- I did it, pépé. I averted the danger and I will bring our family back to greatness.

He stared in silence at the portrait and he spoke after a while:

- No. I will not end sanctions against Eileen Lu. She must fall for opposing me. It is the only way. She must fall in the same way that you brought down our family.

After saying this, Pierre shed a tear, and he recalled the day when his family fell from grace. Pierre's parents and his sister had died in a mountaineering accident. Destroyed by sorrow, Vincent had believed that their deaths were divine punishment for his crimes. To find peace, Vincent had admitted that the family fortune came from Nazi victims during World War 2. After this, the Swiss authorities had seized their assets, Vincent had killed himself, and Pierre had ended up in a foster home.

His fall from grace had convinced Pierre about his true purpose in life, to rise again and bring the Beaumont family back to glory. Pierre had almost reached his goal. He was the wealthiest man in the world, and if he could achieve success with his breeding program, the Beaumont's would rise and rule the world. That was a vision to fight for.

With tear still running down his cheeks, Pierre laughed a burst of hysterical laughter, then cried himself to sleep at night.

Chapter 18: A Sensational Victory, 3rd November 2028.

Eva Moreno was sitting in her campaign headquarters in Santa Fe together with her partner Angela Baker and her brother Andres Moreno. Despite the enthusiastic shouting by her supporters outside, Eva felt heartbroken. Since Eileen Lu had withdrawn her support, Eva had been exposed to relentless media attacks. Most of the attacks against her were absurd and fraudulent reports. However, with media and social media ownership concentrated to a small group, there was nothing she could do. Because of the relentless attacks, Eva's polling had collapsed, and she had fallen from a 40 per cent support level, to a level in the single digits.

Eva felt hollowed watching the exit polls on the television screen. She would lose, despite being the only candidate that actually cared about her fellow citizens. She would lose to a group of plutocrats who would stop at nothing when it came to killing democracy and oppressing their fellow citizen for their personal gains.

Angela hugged Eva and stroke her hair.

- At least you gave them a run for their money, sweetheart. History will remember the independent female candidate that almost ended the political duopoly in the USA.

Eva:

- I want people to remember me for my achievements. Not for being the closest candidate to shake up the status quo.

Andres Moreno:

- Don't say that! You scared those bastards for a while. You riled Pierre Beaumont when you revealed that Reversogene had killed a lot of people.

Eva:

- Yet the exit polls show that Damien Vanderbilt will get 48 per cent of the votes, Barry O'Connor 42 per cent, while I stand at just 8 per cent. I mean come on. Damien is the most corrupt politician in our history of corrupt politicians and Barry doesn't even know what year it is.

Angela:

- I know, love. But let's keep the hope up for now. You should speak to your followers. The night is young, and anything can happen.

Eva:

- You are correct. There can still be a miracle.

PIERRE BEAUMONT WAS following the presidential election in his home in Switzerland. He felt terrified about the outcome. Despite polls showing that Damien would win by a large margin, Pierre couldn't relax. Pierre knew that the polls were fake. Out of fear for a leak, none of his associates had dared to make an accurate poll in the weeks leading up to the election. In the last real poll that they had made four weeks earlier, Eva had maintained a large lead over Damien. Pierre could only hope that the sheepish masses had bought the fake narrative about Damien's popularity.

Pierre's phone rang. It was from Damien. Pierre:

- Hello Damien.

Damien:

- We are fucked! Eva has won in Maine. 46 % to her, 33 % to me, and 18 % to Barry.

Pierre:

- Don't publish the result in media. Instead, publish the article and the scripts about voter fraud. We'll need to delegitimise Eva as much as we can.

Damien:

- Understood. But the electoral college handles counting the votes, not my media empire. No matter what I do, it doesn't change the facts.

Pierre:

- Sow dissent and mistrust in Eva, delay her in the courts. Do everything to discredit her. I will come up with a solution.

- Claim victory at the end of the night regardless of the result.

Having said this, Pierre hung up the phone. In a bout of anger, he threw his phone at his bulletproof window. This shattered the phone but left the window undamaged.

———— ╫╢╢╘╫ ————

EVA MORENO COULDN'T believe her eyes when the election results were published late at night. She had won the presidential election with 42 % of the popular vote, compared to 35 % for Damien Vanderbilt and 18 % for Barry O'Connor. Barry had already conceded his loss and congratulated Eva on her sensational victory. Damien, on the other hand, had released a statement in the news and social media where he accused Eva of voter fraud and stated his intent to take her to court for voter fraud. It didn't matter to Eva.. Damien was desperate for her to lose because he knew that her first presidential order would be to arrest him, as well as Pierre Beaumont, and James Winter for the deaths that Reversogene caused to Americans.

Eva gathered herself and walked out to the stage together with her brother and her partner. She gave a speech to the cheering crowds:

- Today is a historical day. Today is the day when the deep state falls and democracy rises. Despite relentless media attacks in the last months, Damien Vanderbilt could not defeat us. This marks the end of his reign of fake news and propaganda. Yet again, the government should govern for the people and not increase the wealth of a small circle of billionaires.

- My first policy will be to break up the ownership of media and social media and give the rights of freedom of information to everyone at no cost. No longer shall a small group dominate the minds of our citizens, to the detriment of the people.

- My second order will be to file charges against Pierre Beaumont, James Winter and Damien Vanderbilt for the deaths caused by Reversogene. I will also order a full inquiry into the origins of Hei Bai Virus outbreak in New York. I am not satisfied with how that investigation was performed, as there was never a true set of evidence found that it had originated from China's ex-president Jing Xi, as we all have been led to believe.

- Thank you all. May God bless America.

After saying this, Eva walked off the stage and secret service agents took Eva to a secure location. Eva knew that she had put a target on her back by winning the election. Against the men who released unreliable drugs that killed millions, she couldn't be too careful. Eva sighed and reminded herself that once the conspirators were in prison, she could become the president that she strove to be.

Chapter 19: Pierre and James plan to assassinate Eva, 4th November 2028.

Pierre was recovering from a hangover. He had lost his cool upon hearing about Eva's election win, and he had drenched his sorrows with wine and whisky. In that sedated state, he had reached a level of clarity and found the solution that his Zetan monocle couldn't find for him. He would have Eva Moreno murdered, and he would pin the blame on Eileen Lu. While it was absurd that Eileen would murder the president that she helped getting elected, Pierre's plan would work. People were dumb and believed what they were told. In 2020 the media had succeeded in scaring 30-year-olds of a virus, which mostly killed elderly, so he could convince them that China had murdered Eva Moreno.

Pierre summoned James Winter, who came down from the guestroom where he had holed up for the last months.

James gave Pierre a long look. James:

- What is going on, Pierre? You look terribly ill.

Pierre:

- So, would you, if you drank for 36 hours straight in your late fifties. Age, I am telling you, is a merciless beast.

James shook his head and sighed:

- So, do you want something in particular or are you going to entertain me with nonsensical chatter?

Pierre:

- I know what we have to do to get out of our predicament. We must murder Eva Moreno and frame China's president Eileen Lu for the murder.

James:

- That's absolute nonsense. Why would Eileen Lu send someone to murder the president that she helped to win the election? No-one would believe in it.

Pierre:

- You're wrong. To understand lesser men, you must lower your intelligence. During my 36- hour stupor, I saw the truth. Given the attention span of average Americans and their bias towards Chinese people, it will make them believe in our message if we repeat it enough times. Damien controls the media and he will become the next president. People will soon forget about the real reasons behind Eva's death.

James:

- Even so, Damien is not the next in line if Eva dies. Her vice president candidate, Jonathan Xi Feng is next in line.

Pierre:

- Not if we convince people that Xi Feng conspired with China's president to murder Eva. Neither the Republicans nor the Democrats are happy with Eva's election. The congress would be happy to imprison Xi Feng and let Damien Vanderbilt become the President.

James:

- I am not too sure about this plan.

Pierre shrugged his shoulders, poured himself a whiskey, sculled it, and replied:

- What you think is irrelevant. I am your only hope. Eva will prosecute you for treason.

James sighed and replied:

- Whatever. What is the next part of your drunken plan, Pierre?

Pierre:

- We will contact Elaine Orchard from The Harapan Conglomerate to find a suitable hitman with ties to China. Her company operates in South East Asia and she knows the talent pool better than we do. We should also involve Martin Orchard. We need one of our own to make sure that the job gets done while Vladimir is still in a coma.

James:

- Why do we need Martin Orchard? He doesn't bring anything to the table. I can shoot Eva myself.

Pierre:

- I told you I had a plan. You will be with Eva when she dies. We'll make it look like you have defected to her side. Eva will love to attend when you are giving a speech to the press outlining the crimes of Damien Vanderbilt, Vladimir, and me. I want you to pretend to betray me, but before you reveal anything, our Chinese hitman will kill Eva. This will confuse everyone, and we can use this our advantage.

James:

- I see. This could work. I guess you'll short the markets on the day of the assassination?

Pierre:

- Of course. I would never let a crisis go to waste. It is the perfect time to short the markets.

- Now I must retreat to my bedroom. Alcohol abuse has damaged my body, and I cannot achieve my plans if my body perishes. I'll see you tomorrow.

After saying this, Pierre retreated to his bedroom. He took off his monocle, stared at the ceiling, and passed out from being drunk and exhausted.

Chapter 20: Pierre involves Elaine in the Assassination Plans, 6th November 2028.

Pierre felt jittery and nervous as his private jet prepared to land at Jakarta International Airport in Indonesia. The hungover was still encapsulating his head in a thick fog and he abstained from drinking red wine to allow his body to recover. Pierre recognised the tension from when there was an outbreak of the Hei Bai Virus seven years earlier, but this time, there was a major distinction. Back in 2021, Pierre had been an outsider, and the release of the virus which led to the mandatory imposing of the cure was his path to glory. Now he was on the top, so he had everything to lose and nothing more to win. Yet, being on the top, he had to eat or be eaten, and killing Eva Moreno was his only option.

Pierre opened the test profiles of his offspring, Lucien and Delphine, the artificially inseminated end products of his breeding project. They were excellent human specimens that excelled in both intelligence and ruthlessness. Yet, they were only four years old, so Pierre had to succeed in killing Eva for the future of the Beaumont Family. Pierre envisioned how the Beaumont's would rule the world. In his ideal world, all the power and wealth would stay with a small elite, while the ignorant masses existed to serve these rich elites.

Pierre woke up from his daydreaming when the plane touched down. The force of the landing was too much for Pierre and he threw up. He got up and had a hissy fit:

- Jean! Bring a fresh suit for me and tell the pilot that his terrible manoeuvring of the plane made me sick!

Jean nodded and rushed off to get Pierre a spare outfit.
James gave Pierre a curious look and spoke:

- Are you okay, Pierre? Can I be sure that you are up to the task at hand?

Pierre threw his soiled suit jacket to the floor and gave James a cold stare. Pierre:

- Never question me, James. Eva is coming after you as well, so I am your only hope. Never forget that.

James didn't reply. Pierre wasn't his only hope, there was an alternative. He could defect to Eva and sell out the others in return for a presidential pardon. If he did, he could withdraw from the bureau and spend his time being a stepdad to Melinda's children. As Pierre ran off to the back of the plane to freshen up, James called Melinda. She didn't pick up the phone. James sighed. The uncertainty nearly killed him, and all he wanted was an answer to the question that had tormented him for the last month. He needed to know whether there was still hope for their relationship.

ELAINE ORCHARD STARED at the scruffy-looking Pierre Beaumont as he entered the dining hall of her mansion in Jakarta. While Pierre had always been an ugly man, he always strove for a neat and immaculate appearance. Yet, his jacket was wrinkly, his eyes were glary, and he smelled funny. Could Pierre be sick? Elaine decided to voice her concerns:

- Oh dear, Pierre. What happened to you?

Pierre gave Elaine a cold-stare and muttered:

- What kind of question is that? I have faced a lot of stress because of Eva's election victory. You, on the other hand, are not in danger from Eva.

Elaine ignored Pierre's tone of voice and replied:

- Neither are you. Eva has no power to prosecute you in Switzerland.

Pierre shook his head and replied:

- You're wrong. The moment Eva releases an international arrest order for me, my life is over. What would I do then? I can't hide away at Palace Beaumont hoping that the Swiss Government will protect me.

Elaine:

- Well, lucky you know me. I know the perfect man for ending Eva's ambitions.

Having said this, Elaine handed Pierre a folder.

Pierre opened the folder and studied the profile of the assassin. Lim Dao was the perfect candidate for the job. He was a former Taiwanese elite soldier who was currently working as a soldier of fortune. Lim Dao's most important qualification was not his skills, however, but that he had worked with Xi Feng, Eva Moreno's Vice President candidate. If all went to plan, all the evidence would point towards Jonathan Xi Feng as the perpetrator, backed by China and Iran. This would absolve Pierre and Damien of any suspicion in the murder enquiry.

Pierre nodded towards Elaine and spoke:

- This is an excellent candidate, but there is a problem.

Elaine:

- What is that?

Pierre:

- While his skills are impressive and Lim Dao's connection to Xi Feng and China is crucial, he is still just one man. The Secret Service counter-snipers would kill him in a heartbeat before he gets to shoot Eva. We need another person to locate these counter-snipers and kill them before they shoot our Taiwanese assassin.

Elaine sighed and replied:

- Why didn't you tell me about this? I guess I'll have to assemble a whole team, but that creates other problems. How will I conceal my association with a group of mercenaries killing the US president? At least one of them will talk.

Pierre:

- There is a man who would be useful. This man wouldn't get caught, nor speak to the Americans.

Elaine:

- Who is this man?

Pierre:

- Martin Orchard.

Elaine was shocked to hear that and said:

- I doubt that he would be willing to leave Kiribati where he is currently residing. Last time I spoke to him, he was happy sleeping with the housekeeper and writing his god-damn books.

Pierre taunted:

- Do I hear some resentment towards your ex-husband? How unexpected.

Elaine:

- That bastard caused the deaths of hundreds of people when we fought against the Juarez Cartel in Colombia back in 2022. While I am happy to be alive, I can't get rid of the nightmares from witnessing burnt children. Martin's actions burned down the entire Valla de la Muerte valley.

Pierre:

- Then I assume you have no issues if we put him in harm's way?

Elaine:

- No, I don't mind. If you think his participation is necessary to further our goals, then so be it. Do what you must do.

Pierre turned to James and spoke:

- Did you hear that, James? Gather some mercenaries and pay Martin Orchard a visit in Kiribati. A man with his talents shouldn't stay in retirement when we need him.

James nodded and replied:

- Understood. I know some mercenaries in this region. They did some jobs for the CIA a few years ago. Coming in force will convince Martin to be cooperative.

Pierre took out a USB memory with a cryptocurrency account and handed the key to James. Pierre:

- This crypto account should have enough money to cover your expenses. Find Martin and avoid violence, we need him on our side.

James nodded and left the room.
After James had left, Elaine turned towards Pierre and spoke:

- So, do you need to see Lim Dao yourself or should I leave the contact to my head of security, Budi Sepulyat?

Pierre:

- I shall not meet the assassin who will kill the American president. It would be disastrous if we get photographed together. I leave the brutish actions to others, such as James, Vladimir, and Martin. Now, is there anything else?

Elaine:

- Yes, I would like to discuss some of my business projects with you. In full confidence, of course.

Pierre sighed. He didn't believe that such a discussion could be fruitful, but he had to repay Elaine for finding a suitable assassin.
Pierre:

- Very well. Bring in some suitable refreshments and I will share my wealth of knowledge.

Elaine clapped her hands and shouted to her servants:

- Pelayan. Bawalah anggur terbaik dan keju-keju terbaik kami. *(Servants. Bring our best wines and best cheeses for us.)*

As the servant brought the fine wines and produce, Pierre noticed something that lifted his spirits. Elaine's servants had brought a bottle of Domaine Leroy Chambertin Grand Cru 1990 as well as a platter with delicate and exquisite Swiss cheeses. If Elaine preferred the same vintage, their conversation had potential.
Pierre:

- I love your taste in wine. If we share the same shrewdness for commerce, I am sure we will have a fruitful discussion ahead of us.

Elaine smiled to herself. She had done her due diligence and learnt about Pierre's favourite foods and drinks. It was the best way to manipulate a man that was so full of himself. While listening to Pierre's arrogant words was painful, Pierre was her best chance to finance the future of Indonesia that she envisioned. After indulging in the wines and cheeses, Pierre and Elaine spent the night discussing their future business projects.

Chapter 21: James Winter Convinces Martin Orchard to help, 9th November 2028.

James Winter was drinking a glass of beer at a bar overlooking the Pacific Ocean in the sleepy village of Tarawa, which was the capital of Kiribati. The locals looked at him and his entourage with a mix of curiosity and terror. James had hired a group of experienced mercenaries to make sure that Martin Orchard didn't cause any trouble. James and his associates looked menacing in the eyes of the elderly cruise ship passengers that usually visited Kiribati for a vacation.

James sighed. It would have been easier to hire someone else for the assassination, but Martin Orchard was the best hitman there was, in Vladimir's absence. Equipped with the Zetan Monocle set to combat mode, Martin had fought his way out of the captivity of the sadistic drug lord Andres Juarez in Colombia. Martin had annihilated the Juarez drug cartel and torched the entire valley. The fatalities had been in the hundreds and James hoped that history wouldn't repeat itself in Washington.

James' phone rang. It was his ex, Melinda Barnes. Melinda spoke with a direct tone:

- Hi James. I have a message from Eva Moreno. She is willing to give you a presidential pardon, if you reveal the Reversogene cover-up that your co-conspirators did to the world, during a public announcement.

James:

- Since when are you Eva Moreno's mouthpiece?

Melinda:

- I am not. Eva reached out to me knowing that I was in a relationship with you. I am relaying her message.

James:

- Well, are we still in a relationship?

Melinda:

- Don't be silly, James. There is a reason I haven't picked up your calls. I just want to give you the chance to do the right thing.

James:

- Tell her I will do it if she will be attending the public announcement.

Melinda:

- Okay, I will relay your message.

James:

- Thank you.

Melinda:

- James, please be careful. If Pierre or Damien find out about your betrayal, they will come after you.

James:

- Trust me, they won't know. Call me when you have the details.

Melinda:

- Yes. Take care of yourself.

James hung up the phone and a bittersweet feeling overwhelmed him. He had known all along that there was no hope left for him and Melinda, and yet she had called him. On the bright side, this would lure Eva out in the open for the planned assassination, while giving himself an alibi.

'I guess it's time for me to be extravagant with wine and women,' James thought and he walked up to the bar and put down a few $100 bills. James:

- I am looking for female companionship for the night. Preferably a good looking one.

Bartender:

- This venue does not provide this kind of services, you must be mistaken.

James:

- I'm asking you privately. I want someone fresh and young; I am sure $1000 will suffice. It's a yearly pay in Kiribati after all. There is even an added bonus for you if you fulfil my request.

The bartender got on the phone and made some calls. A while later, a cute but somewhat chubby young Gilbertese woman approached James. The young woman stuttered:

- Hi. I am Mawara. My brother said you were looking for company.

James looked at Mawara for a while. He thought of sending her away, but he realised that he wasn't spoiled for choice. James smiled at Mawara and spoke:

- Nice to meet you, Mawara. I am James and these are for you. Please follow me upstairs.

Having said this, James handed Mawara a few banknotes and he led her upstairs.

———— ✝‖⇇ ————

JAMES WINTER FELT CONTENT when he boarded the rented vessel accompanied by his mercenary entourage. While Mawara hadn't been a talented lover, she had been a virgin and James hadn't experienced sex with a virgin for many years. As he took Mawara's virginity, he felt reborn. He had overcome the infatuation and yearning for Melinda that had plagued him for the last months.

On the boat ride to Martin's secluded island, James was pretending to be friends with the Persian jihadist, Ervin Ghorbani. James planned to turn Ervin into a scapegoat, by killing him. There was nothing personal about murdering Ervin. However, killing the Persian jihadist and placing his dead body at Martin's shooting site would deflect the responsibility for the death of Eva Moreno. Once he had successfully framed America's biggest enemies, no-one would think of looking elsewhere for the perpetrators.

As James spoke to Ervin, he realised that they were alike, and James felt excited knowing that he would be the master of Ervin's fate. After what felt like a heartbeat, the boat arrived at Martin Orchard's mansion, which faced a secluded atoll.

MARTIN ORCHARD WAS writing one of his novels when James and his men arrived. Martin heard the boat's engine and decided to walk down to the jetty. At first, he hoped that his housekeeper and mistress, Alani, had come to visit him. While she wasn't rostered this day, he wished she would come because he liked her company. Martin sighed when he realised that his visitor was James Winter, accompanied by a group of shady operatives.

James spotted Martin and commanded:

- So, this is where you are hiding, Martin? Get on the boat! We got a job for you to do.

Martin paused and checked his monocle. It read: *'Combat mode: Odds for survival less than 2 %. The suggested course of action: Compliance.'*
Martin sighed:

- It doesn't seem like I have much of a choice, do I?

James smirked:

- That's correct, Martin. That's why I brought others to deter you from resorting to violence.

Martin:

- Okay, I am coming with you. However, there is something I need to do first.

James taunted:

- What would that be? You have lived alone and off the grid for two years.

Martin:

- I need to write a letter to my housekeeper, Alani. I will give her the house and access to my Kiribati bank account. She needs them more than I do.

James:

- Very well. Hurry up, I don't like waiting.

Martin didn't respond, and he retreated to his home office. After writing the note to Alani, Martin grabbed both his fake and real passports and walked to the jetty without a word.

As the ship took off, James had to contain his doubt of Martin's trustworthiness. While James surrounded himself with shady characters, Martin was the only one who posed a threat to him. *'Remember that this is the first day of the big plan!'* James mumbled to himself, leaned back into his seat, and fell asleep.

Chapter 22: The Assassination of Eva Moreno, 12th November 2028.

James felt nervous as he exited the private jet accompanied by Martin Orchard and his group of mercenaries. It was crucial that there was no record of James being in the same flight as the others in case border officials detained some of them. 'Is everything going as planned?' Pierre sent this hologram message to James via the Zetan Monocle. 'Yes.' James replied.

James had discussed their plan to go back to the USA with Pierre. They didn't want to attract any attention to themselves, but they didn't want it to be too shady either. Their solution was to hack the border customs at the private Washington airport where they landed. To the unknowing operator, everything looked in order, but none of the information were saved or sent to the database, so none of these mercenaries were recorded to have entered the country. "Welcome home, Mr Winter," an immigration officer said, and James felt how a big weight had fallen off his shoulders.

James was safe for now. He had lost his job, but the American president Mitchell Cent had banned all investigations into James' conduct and connections. James glanced at his mercenaries as they passed immigration. While Pierre had hacked the system, there was always a risk that some overzealous immigration officer would go beyond his or her duty. Satisfied that everyone passed immigration without incident, James turned to Martin and spoke:

- Martin, I have some preparations to make. Head to the Jefferson Hotel. I have booked a suite for you there.

Martin gave James a sceptical look and replied:

- Did you book it under my real name? You haven't told me why I am needed and why I had to leave Kiribati.

James:

- I booked your room in your real name. Your mission will not take place at the hotel, so there is no need to use a fake identity.

Martin:

- You still didn't answer the more important question. Why am I here?

James:

- You are here to do a job for the group. You owe us big time, since Pierre and I resurrected you after your silly escapade in Colombia.

Martin:

- Why won't you tell me?

James:

- Well, it is easier to learn something correctly the first time than to unlearn incorrect knowledge. Thus, I won't brief you until our plan is complete.

- I suggest that you head to your hotel. I have some things to deal with before briefing you.

After saying this, James got into a cab and ordered a ride back to his Washington home.

JAMES WINTER FELT EXHAUSTED returning to the home he hadn't been to since Eva Moreno exposed his involvement of the Reversogene cover-up. The house itself meant nothing to James, but it felt good to have roots to a place again. James had hated staying in Pierre's mansion, but it had been for the best. There were still independent media sources around, and they would have made James' life a nightmare if he had stayed in the USA. In his absence, the press had moved on to other more present topics than deaths that occurred seven years earlier.

James tried to focus on the task at hand, but he couldn't. The house was too messy and full of dust, after being unoccupied for four months. The pictures of Melinda and her children hanging on the walls made James feel resentful and heartbroken. She had betrayed him, and he needed to clear every trace of her out of his life. James wanted Melinda to be one of the people that took the fall for Eva Moreno's murder. He called Pierre:

- I have an additional objective I would like to add to the mission.

Pierre:

- I don't like last-minute changes. Why didn't you mention this before?

James:

- Nevertheless, it needs to happen. I want to frame Melinda for being the mole who sold us the positions of the Secret Service counter snipers.

There was a silence for a while. Eventually, Pierre replied:

- Have you organised the meeting with Eva Moreno yet?

James:

- Not yet.

Pierre:

- Then you should do that first.

- Don't worry, I will help you with your pointless revenge against your ex. I will make a few deposits into Melinda's account that appears to come from the Iranian government. Then, I will leak this information to the press.

- Now get back to what's important, Eva Moreno's assassination.

After saying this, Pierre hung up the phone.

James felt bad for going after Melinda after he made his request, and he had hoped that Pierre would refuse, but he couldn't change his mind again. James called Eva Moreno's aide, Aaron Smith, to set up a meeting. After that, he left his house to get away from all his old memories.

JAMES WINTER FELT INSTANT disdain when he met Aaron Smith at a fancy coffee shop. Aaron was an effeminate politician with purple hair, and James couldn't respect a man like that. In the end, it didn't matter. James hadn't come to join Eva Moreno but to draw her into a trap.

Aaron smiled at James and spoke:

- Welcome home, James. Thank you for reaching out. Would you like some coffee? The caramel hazelnut affogato is divine.

'Fucking hell, Pierre's homosexuality is bad enough!' James thought to himself, but he contained his homophobia and replied:

- A large cup of extra strong black coffee. No sugar.

Aaron exclaimed:

- Oh, how masculine. I'll be right back!

A short while later, Aaron returned with their beverages and James spoke:

- So, why the diversion with the coffee? Let's discuss our deal.

Aaron chuckled:

- Of course. Let's do business.

- Eva is happy to pardon you if you give up your co-conspirators during a public announcement.

James:

- Will Eva Moreno herself attend?

Aaron:

- I cannot guarantee it. Eva is a busy woman and she needs to prepare for her presidency.

James taunted:

- I doubt she'll pass up on the chance to gloat in the defeat of the man she referred to as an enemy of humanity.

Aaron:

- Eva doesn't gloat in the defeat of her enemies. Eva wants to create a better world for her fellow humans. People suffering the consequences of their actions is a necessary evil.

James thought of arguing back but he realised that he wouldn't do himself any favours criticising Eva. Instead, he changed the topic.

- So, when, and where shall I make the announcement? I am ready to dob in Pierre and Damien.

Aaron:

- I am not at liberty to say. The safety of the president-elect is paramount.

James:

- I have agreed to make a public announcement revealing Pierre and Damien's involvements in the Reversogene cover-up that killed many Americans in response to the Hei Bai virus. I will travel to the meeting on my own accord, but that will only happen if you tell me the time and place well in advance.

Aaron sighed and replied:

- Okay. How about making your public announcement at the steps of the Holocaust Museum on Friday at noontime? The Hei Bai Virus outbreaks and the Reversogene deaths were deliberate and cruel attacks on humankind, so the symbolism is clear.

James nodded and replied:

- Very well. I will be there. Enjoy your coffee, Mr Smith.

Having said this, James got up and left the cafeteria.

JAMES WINTER WAS SITTING in a boardroom in a Washington DC office complex. He felt tense and he hoped that the meeting with Damien would yield the desired outcome. The media needed to deflect all the allegations in the right direction.

Damien Vanderbilt looked sceptical towards James, as he told him about his plan. Damien:

- What if this is a trap? What if they are testing us? What if Eva won't show up?

James shrugged his shoulders and replied:

- In that case, I won't tell them anything. I don't have any credibility to lose, but Eva will look like an idiot for summoning the press conference.

Damien:

- I am worried that they will come after us for Eva's murder.

James:

- Why worry? It's a perfect setup. Neither the Democrats nor the Republicans want to end their political duopoly. So, everyone will accept the fake evidence blaming Eva's vice president-elect, Jonathan Xi Feng, for her assassination and you will become America's president.

Damien:

- What if you're wrong?

James:

- Pierre and I have thought of this plan very carefully. If we manipulate the news to divert people's attention, the nation will focus on other issues than following through with Eva's crusade against us. In any case, the situation can't get worse from eliminating Eva.

Damien:

- So, what do you want me to do?

James:

- As the news mogul, I want you to divert people's attention and release plenty of propaganda to create mass confusion. I will deal with the murders.

Damien:

- Understood. I agree that it is better if we focus on our strengths.

James didn't reply. It had been a while since he murdered someone. While his conscience didn't torment him, the concept of conspiring against the future

US president was a stressful ordeal. Not keen to continue the conversation, James Winter left the meeting.

IT WAS FRIDAY AND THE time was 10 AM, two hours before the assassination of Eva were to take place. James Winter was sitting in a shady warehouse belonging to the White Brotherhood leader Randy "Hitler" McNeill. While James didn't like far-right white supremacists, Randy was his best bet for finding a prospective ally for the assassination.

James studied the inbred redneck opposite him. He had to hide his contempt for the man who lived in the century-old myth that one's race made him superior. He knew that it was a man's action that made him superior, not the colour of his skin. If someone could only claim superiority because of racial heritage, it proved that he was insecure and inferior. Randy spoke:

- So, you want to put a bullet in that bitch's head? How can the White Brotherhood help?

James thought about putting a bullet in Randy's head, and claim him to be the second shooter. James stopped himself. While framing the white supremacy movement for Eva's murder was an entertaining scenario, it was not what he had agreed with Pierre and Damien. James said:

- I need you to move the body of someone.

Randy:

- Who?

James:

- You'll soon find out.

A door opened and the Persian jihadist Ervin Ghorbani entered the warehouse. He looked at James and Randy in confusion and spoke:

- Hey, Mr Winter. Why are we meeting in this shithole?

Randy clenched his teeth and growled:

- Why the fuck did you bring the dirty sand nigger to my place?

James turned around and shot Ervin between the eyes with a silenced pistol. After that, he chucked his pistol to the floor, turned around, and smirked at Randy. James said:

> - I want you to dump his body at a certain location. Take him to
> the roof of the Artisan Condominium building and hide him out of
> sight until I say so. Here is a cryptocurrency account with payment
> for your troubles.

Having said this, James handed Randy a USB-drive with cryptocurrency details. After this, he left the room while the flabbergasted Randy stared at him.

JAMES WINTER WAS FEELING tense as he stepped out on the podium that was set in front of the main entrance to the Holocaust Museum. His monocle showed that Lim Dao, the assassin that was tasked to shoot Eva; Martin Orchard, who was tasked to shoot the American counter-snipers; and the American snipers were all in positions, but where was Eva? James walked up to the podium, looked at the crowd, and set his monocle to 'improvise and delay speech'. For what felt like an eternity, James was reading up gibberish that his monocle fed him to the public, lengthy eulogies to people he didn't even know about, while waiting for Eva's appearance.

Eventually, Eva arrived, walked up to James, put her hand on his shoulder, and spoke:

> - I appreciate the touching tributes, but perhaps you should tell the
> press why you are here?

'Proceed now!' James sent this message to Martin via his monocle. His monocle entered 'time mode' and James perception of time slowed down. Martin shot the American counter-snipers at the same time the assassin Lim Dao pulled the trigger towards Eva from afar. Time slowed down to a standstill, when Lim Dao was hit in the exact moment he shot towards Eva.

'Danger, Danger. Incoming .50 calibre bullet is coming towards you.' The monocle beeped. *"Oh shit! Lim Dao shot towards me by mistake!"* James thought frantically.

James acted decisively. Still having his 'time mode' on his monocle, he faked a slippage while also dragging Eva's helpless body into the position where he had stood. James perception of time resumed, and he fell headfirst to the floor. James' nose cracked as his head hit the pavement and blood splashed into his eyes.

As James got up, he looked at what remained of Eva. The heavy-calibre bullet had left a huge gaping wound in her head, and her blood had splattered across the stage. Her assistant Aaron Smith had got hit by the bullet, which had taken off a few of his skinny fingers, and he screamed in agony. 'Serves the poof right!' James thought to himself and smiled before he faked fainting from his deliberate slippage.

Chapter 23: Pierre frames Jonathan Xi Feng and Eileen Lu for Eva's murder, 15th November 2028.

Pierre Beaumont wasn't bothered by the chilling wind that met his face when he exited his private jet onto the tarmac of a tiny airport in Washington DC. He felt more alive than he had felt for years, and everything was set up for success. Everything had gone exactly as he had planned. The counter-snipers killing Lim Dao had tied up a loose end and ensured that Lim would not be a future threat. Pierre had organised transactions to make it appear like China's Eileen Lu had paid Jonathan Xi Feng, Eva Moreno's vice president elect, who then hired Lim Dao and his supposed Persian accomplice, Ervin Ghorbani.

James Winter approached Pierre at the tarmac. James:

- What's with that big grin of yours? It's fucking freezing today.

Pierre:

- A small breeze will not take the joy out of our victory. My victory!

James:

- We are not there yet. An autopsy will reveal that Ervin Ghorbani died hours before the shooting, making him an invalid decoy.

Pierre:

- Yes, I know. But what will they make of it? It will suit the Republicans and the Democrats to keep their duopoly and follow our narrative. Damien's media will discredit Ervin's autopsy report and the coroner will fall in line.

James:

- What about accusations that I might be involved in this plot? People have been talking about the strange coincidence that I slipped just before the shooting and managed to drag Eva right into the path of the bullet.

Pierre:

- It's inconsequential. Evidence shows that China's Eileen Lu and her puppet Xi Feng had paid Lim Dao to carry out the shooting. If they intended to shoot you but shot the president by mistake, that wouldn't make a difference from a legal point of view.

- But do tell me, how did you anticipate the trajectory of the bullet with enough accuracy to get Eva into the right spot?

James:

- The monocle warned me and slowed down my perception of time.

Pierre:

- I see. These Zetan Monocles are impressive gadgets, aren't they?

James:

- Martin's story was even more impressive, albeit impossible. He claimed that he shot Lim's bullet mid-air to change the trajectory of the bullet towards Eva.

Pierre:

- That's absurd. Our friend Martin was only tasked to shoot the counter-snipers protecting her.

James:

- He needs a new purpose. I've sent him to Israel to help the Yehuda Brothers open the gate that blocks the primordial Zeto Crystal.

Pierre:

- Good plan. I will pay him a visit. But first, we need to meet Damien and congratulate him on his unorthodox way of winning the presidency.

Having said this, Pierre and James entered a limousine that took them to Damien's Washington DC mansion.

DAMIEN'S MANSION DIDN't impress Pierre. He had hoped that a fellow billionaire would have an impressive dwelling full of exquisite furniture and expensive artwork, but Damien's newly renovated abode showed an extreme lack of taste.

Damien sensed Pierre's disapproval and he spoke:

- I am sorry for the state of my Washington mansion. I have focused too much of my efforts on creating presentable mansions in New York, the Hamptons, and the Bahamas.

Pierre:

- Don't worry. You'll soon have the most impressive dwelling of them all, The Whitehouse. The seat of power for the Western World.

Damien smirked:

- Well, the real power lies elsewhere.

Pierre:

- Yes. Yet, you'll control the armed goons and the drone strikes. With you in the Whitehouse, we can spread chaos without the fear of repercussions.

Damien:

- We are not there yet. Xi Feng's trial hasn't been finalised, and he might still get Eva's electoral votes if he can prove himself innocent.

Pierre shrugged his shoulders and replied:

- Well, that's where you come in. I need you to convince other American politicians that they need to sentence Xi Feng for treason and for you to become the president. It's in their self-interests, so it should be an easy sell.

Damien:

- I need some help with that.

Pierre smiled:

- That's why I am here. When big money talks, politicians listen.

Damien:

- Thank you, Pierre.

Pierre shook his head:

- Don't thank me, Damien. My support comes at a steep price. But not for you. Now let's sit down and discuss how I envision the future of America.

Damien clapped his hands and a servant came in. Damien:

- Please bring us food and drinks, Mr Beaumont has travelled far and needs refreshments.

As Pierre tasted the wine and food, he had to hide his irritation. Damien had done a lousy job researching Pierre's culinary preferences. Pierre faked a smile. While the wine tasted off, control over the US army and drone fleet were within his grasp, so there was no reason to cry over sour grapes. Pierre:

- Thank you very much for this exquisite dinner. Now let's discuss my vision on how to further the progress of the human species.

Chapter 24: Massive protests force Eileen Lu to resign, 2nd December 2028.

E ileen Lu looked at the crowds that had gathered on Tianmen Square. The table had been turned. Tianmen Square, once a place of reverence where her countrymen had stood up against the tyranny of the Columnist Party, was now a place where people stood up against her. Eileen Lu studied the masses that had gathered outside. Millions of Chinese citizens had resisted the icy winter winds and they were screaming derogatory terms about her.

Thin lines of riot police surrounded the palace. They would not be enough to protect Eileen if the demonstrations turned violent. Eileen hesitated, she could not bring in the army to disperse the protesters by shooting the innocents, it was not who she was.

The Chinese economy had struggled for years since Eileen Lu became the president. Initially, people had cherished the prospect of being free from the Columnist Party's tyranny. Yet, as the economy deteriorated due to Eileen's refusal to bow her head to the international banking regulations, people had turned against her. The last straw was the allegations that Eileen had financed the assassination of Eva Moreno, to make the American-Chinese Jonathan Xi Feng the president of the USA. The allegations were unfounded, and Eileen hadn't even met with Xi Feng. Jonathan's Chinese heritage was coincidental, but the rest of the world saw his ethnicity and assumed that he was a Chinese spy.

In the end, it didn't matter. The truth was of no consequence when fighting against villains like Pierre and Damien. Eileen knew she had lost. China was under a complete blockade from the rest of the world. Governments had frozen Chinese assets and deported Chinese citizens. War, both civil and foreign, was brewing unless Eileen Lu stepped down.

Min Li entered Eileen's office and spoke:

- Special Agent Min Li, reporting for duty.

Eileen gave her a resigned look and replied:

- Do you have any good news? Please tell me there is a way out of this.

Min Li:

- I fear not. I suspect the riot police will abandon you. If that happens, anything can happen. People are blaming their hardship on your involvement in US politics.

Eileen sighed. Helping Eva Moreno had been a crucial mistake. Eileen had shared Eva's convictions about stopping Pierre and the other powerbrokers that governed from the shadows. Eva was dead, and Eileen would follow in her footsteps unless she could figure something out.
Eileen pleaded to Min Li:

- Please don't let the mob catch me. Shoot me if you must.

Min Li:

- Don't say that. There is still hope.

Eileen:

- What kind of hope? I crushed the Columnist Party and I rejected the banking cabal. But the population are destitute and there is no relief in sight. I can't tyrannise the population I am meant to serve. Even if I wanted to, I don't have the army's support.

Min Li:

- Go into exile. The Emir of Dubai is offering you political asylum.

Eileen:

- Would the Americans agree to that? They allege that I killed their president.

Min Li:

- They know you didn't. It's a political play to stop reform from happening. Eva winning the election threatened the corrupt career politicians that have feathered their nests for too long.

Eileen:

- I guess I have no choice. I'll call Emir Aksam Al-Islam straight away.

Eileen got on the phone with Emir Aksam and after a short conversation, she turned to Min Li.
Eileen:

- He accepted me and offered me asylum. I will take you to Dubai as my protector.

Min Li:

- Understood, President Lu. It will be an honour to keep serving you.

Eileen:

- Glad to hear that. Let's head to the helicopter on the roof. We need to leave.

Eileen and Min Li rushed to the helicopter that took them to a secret army base for further transport out of the country. As Eileen watched the masses that had gathered against her rule, she felt heartbroken. Her life of good intentions had pawed her way to hell, and her only option was to flee like a criminal. How would she recover from this?

Eileen thought of Jared Pond. He broke her heart when he left her after she took out her vengeance on the Columnist Party politicians when she became China's leader. Jared was right all along. Eileen had been a great inspiration as a freedom fighter and dissenter against Chairman Jing Xi's tyranny. Yet, her tenure at the presidency could be characterised by incompetence at best, and tyranny at worst. Eileen sighed and she hoped she would see Jared one day in the future.

Their helicopter reached the airport. Eileen and Min Li rushed towards a plane that took them out of China, never to return.

Chapter 25: President Damien Vanderbilt writes the Monocle Conspiracy a blank check, 2nd February 2029.

Josefina Fiero was enjoying Caipirinhas in the shade of a rubber tree in the park surrounding her Brazilian palace. Her adopted daughter Sandra Santiago and her friend Elaine Orchard accompanied her. They were gossiping and sharing stories about men and beauty treatments. A heavy burden had been lifted off her chest the day Damien Vanderbilt became the US president. Damien had called his Brazilian counterpart, Jorge Santacruz, and the allegations against Josefina's business empire had disappeared. Josefina had considered going after Jorge, but she had refrained from doing so. Jorge had made himself look like a fool, and that in itself was a victory.

Josefina smiled towards Elaine and spoke:

- So, is Martin coming to our meeting?

Elaine:

- No, Martin and Szymon Yehuda are looking for a Zeto Crystal hidden somewhere around Lake Victoria in Africa. Martin claims that there is a Zetan Temple on Nabuyongo Island that is visible only once every 12 years.

Josefina:

- Such a waste of time looking for these ancient crystals when we can achieve so much if we work together for a worthwhile cause.

Elaine:

- I disagree. You must remember that our primary goal is to find and utilise the power of the primordial Zeto crystal. Even a replicated Zeto Crystal could power the monocles to their utmost supreme conditions, and the crystals even brought Martin back from the dead in 2022. Imagine the powers that lie within the primordial Zeto Crystal, the true ancient Zetan source of energy in this universe.

Josefina:

- So, what would you do if you got your hands on that crystal?

Elaine paused for a while to think before she replied:

- I wouldn't get my hands on it. I am not pursuing it; hence I am here.

Josefina:

- Yet you know more than me about the pursuit for the Zeto Crystal.

Elaine:

- It came up during my last conversation with Martin. I am happy that Martin found a purpose in life again. Now he can pursue his goal to 'stop the apocalypse'.

Josefina:

- The apocalypse that allegedly will take place in 2131, according to a Zetan artefact? What a joke, none of us will be around by then.

Elaine:

- Correct. But like religion, it gives a far-away purpose in life. I am happy for him. I would like to find God.

Josefina:

- What will you do if you don't find a higher purpose?

Elaine:

- I'll turn Indonesia into the greatest nation on Earth, built according to my visions. No poverty, no illness, no suffering.

Josefina:

- That's an unrealistic dream. It will never happen.

Elaine:

- Well, that's my ambition. If we convince the US president Damien Vanderbilt to give us unlimited funding, it can happen.

Elaine and Josefina looked towards the helicopter pad, as a US helicopter landed. President Damien Vanderbilt and his family disembarked.
Josefina:

- Damien Vanderbilt has landed, let's host a reception for him.

THE US PRESIDENT DAMIEN Vanderbilt, his first-lady Eloise, and his children Jane and Jeff approached Josefina as they arrived at her mansion. Josefina bit her lip in frustration. She had planned to seduce Damien to get herself advantages, but the presence of his family was a no go. As if Damien read her mind, he spoke:

- Thank you for having us, Josefina. We met with the Brazilian president and my advisors told me that it was beneficial to bring my family on my first overseas trip as a president.

Josefina:

- I didn't even know you had a family. You have never mentioned them before.

Damien:

- Don't be silly. An American President must have a family. That they loathe each other is of no concern.

First lady Eloise interrupted Damien:

- Can I take the children somewhere else? I have no interest in socialising with your latest play toy.

Damien:

- Mind your manner, Eloise. You might be my wife but you're not immune from the dangers in life. Quite the opposite!

Eloise was about to rush off when Damien interrupted her:

- Hold on, we need a happy family photo first. Josefina and Sandra, please join us for a photo.

Eloise sighed and moments later the presidential photographer had snapped some unnatural-looking photos for the Whitehouse propaganda channel. Eloise:

- Come, children, let's head to an amusement park while your father is discussing business with our fabulous host.

The children came to their mother, and moments later they left in a limousine. Josefina smirked:

- Woah, what a happy family you got there!

Damien ignored her tone and stated:

- The nuclear family is crucial for national morale. The family members hating each other is better left unsaid.

Josefina:

- Perhaps you should try to fix your relationship with your wife?

Damien shrugged his shoulders and replied:

- My wife cannot expect that a man in my position must choose between family life and other women. I can and will have both.

After hearing this, Josefina scratched her plan of seducing Damien. It had been an interesting prospect to have sex with the US president, yet his misogynism was a turn-off. Josefina gave Damien a cold stare and spoke:

- We will meet in the dining room when the others have arrived. My servants will look after your every need in the meantime.

Having said this, Josefina turned around and walked back into her mansion.

A WHILE LATER, EVERYONE had gathered in the dining room for an eight-course degustation menu. Present were Josefina Fiero, Sandra Santiago, Pierre Beaumont, Elaine Orchard, Ben Yehuda, James Winter, and Damien Vanderbilt. Damien was in a great mood and he proclaimed:

- I would like to thank you all for your contributions on my path to the presidency. As the US president, I have signed an executive order protecting James and Pierre from the Reversogene drug investigation. I have also agreed with the Brazilian president to stop his unjustified crusade against our gracious host Josefina. I have decided to reinstate James Winter as the CIA director for his outstanding efforts for my country. Finally, I have ordered that your respective companies should be preferred suppliers for US purchases in your regions. This will grant you lucrative opportunities.

Josefina:

- How did you deal with Jorge Santacruz?

Damien:

- I hinted that an Amazon-based indigenous rebel-group was under-way to steal a US drone to kill him. I offered him the deactivation code for a price.

Sandra:

- So, you issued a death threat to our president?

Damien:

- Quite the contrary. I saved his life. It wasn't my fault we lost the drone in the first place. At least that would be difficult to prove.

Pierre:

- I like what I am hearing. Access to the US satellite and drone net-work will be a fantastic way to make troublemakers fall into line.

Damien:

- Yes, and with James Winter reinstated as the CIA director, we will find and eliminate these troublemakers pre-emptively.

James nodded and smirked. Damien continued:

- And to the rest of you, as US government preferred suppliers your business success is guaranteed. You'll become even more prominent than you already are.

- Cheers to my election victory and the future society we will build together.

After Damien finished his speech, everyone cheered. They spent the rest of the day wining and dining while dividing the world amongst themselves.

Chapter 26: Szymon Yehuda gives Pierre a Zeto Crystal. 12th February 2029

Pierre Beaumont exited his private jet at Tel Aviv International airport. He scoffed at what he saw. How could this impoverished desert be the most contested territory in the history of humankind? Yet Pierre knew that deep under the Solomon Temple lay his destiny. If he could get his hands on the primordial Zeto Crystal, the future was his.

Pierre had witnessed the miracles of the replicated Zeto Crystals in the past. These Zetan artifacts could bring back the dead and power up the hidden technologies in Zetan temples. Yet, these crystals were replicas, mass-produced like batteries by the Zetans themselves. The Primordial Zeto Crystal was the original. It was a true source of power and Pierre's Zetan Monocle informed him that he could gain immortality if he found it.

"Welcome to Israel."

Pierre turned around and he saw Szymon Yehuda and Martin Orchard. Szymon had a fresh scar across his face, and Martin had his hand in a gypsum cast.

Pierre:

  - Did you find the Zeto Crystal?

Szymon:

  - Yes, but we almost died. The Temple's defences caused the island to collapse and drowned several members of our entourage.

Pierre knew about this. The collapse of Nabuyongo Island had caused several hundred deaths in Tanzania the previous week. The media narrative had claimed that an earthquake caused the collapse, and no-one had questioned the narrative. Life was cheap and plentiful when it happened in faraway destitute countries.

Pierre:

- The collapse of Nabuyongo Island is of no concern. Quite the opposite. Helping people after natural disasters is an easy way for the World Bank to maintain positive public relations.

Martin snarked:

- Even when the World Bank's actions cause the natural disaster that you're alleviating?

Pierre smirked:

- Who would ever believe in such far-fetched theories? Now take me to the Templar Tunnels and the gateway that blocks the primordial Zeto Crystal. I want to succeed where you fail.

Szymon:

- Of course. Come with us, Pierre.

PIERRE SENSED AN IMMENSE power behind the indestructible gateway that blocked the primordial Zeto Crystal. Pierre, Szymon, and Martin were in the Templar Tunnels, far below the ancient Solomon Temple. This was it. When Pierre deciphered the code, he would become the most powerful man in history.

Pierre turned to Szymon and spoke:

- I guess this is it? Once I decipher the code, no one will be able to stand against us. You'll get your pure-breed Jewish nation, I will attain full global economic control, and Martin will get a chance to stop the future apocalypse.

Szymon nodded and showed off an evil grin. Szymon:

- Of course. We have a deal.

Pierre:

- Very well. Hand me the crystal and tell me how to activate the panels on the wall.

Szymon handed Pierre the replicated Zeto Crystal and spoke:

- Slam the replicated crystal in the hollow section of that wall. That will drain the replica and energise the temple and the control panel.

Pierre nodded, took the crystal, and was about to slam it into the wall when he received a message from his monocle. If he tried to get the primordial Zeto Crystal today, he would fail. There were two potential outcomes if Pierre tried to open the door. Either he would fail, get electrocuted and lose the replicated Zeto crystal as Martin, Szymon, and Ben had fared when they tried to open the door. Or worse yet, if he managed to open the door, he was at the mercy of Szymon and Martin. Pierre was the oldest and least accomplished fighter in the group. If it came to violence between the three of them, he was likely to perish.

Pierre put the replicated Zeto crystal in his pocket and turned around. Szymon ran up to him and shouted:

- What are you doing, Pierre? What is the meaning of this?

Pierre:

- I cannot open the door. Only Keila Eisenstein can open it.

Szymon:

- Keila Eisenstein? Who the hell is that?

Pierre:

- Ask Martin Orchard, or as you call him, Martin Al-Sham. Quite a fitting name for such a duplicitous liar.

Martin:

- I don't know what you are talking about.

Pierre:

- Yes, you do. You searched the CIA archives and you asked your fellow Templar Michael to help you look for her. This happened after you failed to open the gateway. You must have reasons to believe that Keila Eisenstein is the key to opening that door.

Martin:

- I don't know who Keila Eisenstein is. I just know that the name is of importance.

Pierre:

- Bah, you know more than you're willing to admit.

Martin looked away and didn't reply. Szymon looked at Pierre and spoke:

- So, what happens now?

Pierre:

- I will continue funding your operations if you let me leave with this Zeto crystal. With a bit of luck, you'll find this Keila Eisenstein during your travels.

Szymon:

- So, what are you going to do?

Pierre:

- I am going to visit an old friend capable of furthering our cause.

Szymon froze and examined his odds. If he were to enter combat mode: The monocle displayed: *'Odds for survival 43 %. Odds for finding the primordial Zeto Crystal 0.2%.'*
Pierre smirked:

- Do you like those odds, Szymon? Your odds of survival are better than mine, but it won't help you reach your goals.

Szymon didn't reply and Pierre swiftly left the tunnels. Martin approached Szymon and spoke:

- So, what do we do now? Why did you let him leave?

Szymon growled:

- Because you would turn hostile if I attacked Pierre. Besides, why didn't you tell me about Keila Eisenstein?

Martin looked away and stayed silent. Szymon shouted:

- Just what I thought. You better pull yourself together, Al-Sham. I'll debrief you about this later.

Having said this, Szymon strode towards the exit and left Martin Orchard, also known as Martin Al-Sham behind, to yearn for the primordial Zeto crystal, which was so close, yet so far away.

Chapter 27: Pierre resurrects Vladimir and reveals his plan for humanity. 15th February 2029.

Pierre was in a top-secret research lab in Switzerland. Pierre watched Vladimir who was still in a coma, connected to a respirator. Pierre walked up to the doctor who oversaw Vladimir's health and spoke:

- Do you have any news about our patient, Dr Gruber?

Erik Gruber shrugged his shoulders and replied:

- There is nothing new to discuss. The patient is brain dead and beyond hope. Why are you hiring me when there is nothing I can do?

Pierre:

- I wouldn't know that there was nothing you could do if I hadn't hired you to save him. Besides, I pay you a handsome salary, so quit standing around doing nothing.

Erik:

- I wasn't complaining Monsieur Beaumont, I was merely asking.

Pierre:

- In any case, your services are no longer required. I have terminated your employment and I will pay your redundancy according to your employment contract.

Erik:

- May I ask what you are planning to do with the patient?

Pierre:

- You may not. As you are no longer my employee, I urge you to leave my facility at once. My employees will send your belongings to your designated address.

Erik:

- But Mr Beaumont. I have unfinished projects. If I had known, I could have prepared a handover to my colleagues.

Pierre:

- If you had known, you could have stolen research data and prepared to betray me.

Pierre clapped his hands and two beefed-up security guards entered the room.

- Guards, please escort Dr Gruber to the exit and organise the audit and delivery of his belongings.

The guards nodded, grabbed Erik, and led him out of the room.

Pierre smirked. While he didn't distrust Erik, he didn't want him to steal any medical journals, which could have happened if Pierre notified him in advance. Pierre wanted to keep Vladimir's recovery a secret, as the world wasn't ready to know about the Zeto crystals.

Pierre connected Vladimir's monocle to Vladimir's right eye. As per usual, it wasn't enough to bring Vladimir back to consciousness.

Pierre then placed a replicated Zeto crystal on top of Vladimir's monocle. There was a bright flash of immense blue light, and seconds later, Vladimir opened his eyes and took a terrified gasp of air.

Vladimir:

- What happened?

Pierre smiled and said:

- You tell me. How was the world's greatest assassin outdone by a single woman?

Pierre knew the answer; Elaine Orchard had tipped Julienne Bessange on how to outsmart the monocle's AI. Pierre didn't intend to tell Vladimir. If Vladimir killed Elaine, Pierre would lose control over Asia and Martin Orchard would come after them.
Vladimir:

- I don't remember.
- Where is Julienne Bessange now? I must kill her to get my revenge.

Pierre:

- Julienne Bessange is dead. James Winter shot her in the head with a sniper rifle.

Vladimir:

- What about Julienne Bessange's body?

Pierre:

- Dead and cremated. You have been gone for seven months, Vladimir. A lot has happened in your absence.

Vladimir:

- Like what?

Pierre:

- We overthrew Eileen Lu as the president of China. I allowed the Emir of Dubai to take her in. Eileen must live in shame for defying us.

- Eva Moreno won the US presidential election and threatened to put us on trial for our crimes. This was unacceptable, so we killed her and blamed it on China and Iran. My friend Damien Vanderbilt is doing my bidding in the Whitehouse instead.

- Lucien and Delphine, the children born via my breeding program are showing enormous potential to become successful heirs to the Beaumont family. But they are still children and need more training before they are useful.

Vladimir:

- These are all good news. So why did you bring me back?

Pierre smirked:

- Because of my love for your great personality. Why do you ask?

Vladimir gave Pierre a dead stare and replied:

- Tell me the real reason.

Pierre sighed:

- I need your help to secure the primordial Zeto Crystal. I was close to finding it, but I realised that Szymon Yehuda or Martin Orchard would kill me the moment I opened the locked passageway. I need you to be by my side to stop them from getting any dumb ideas.

Vladimir:

- And what will happen once you have the primordial Zeto Crystal?

Pierre:

- With the power of the primordial Zeto Crystal, we will be immortal. Our breeding program will breed new generations of intelligent

superhumans, formed in our image. We will change humanity forever. We will become gods!

After saying this, Pierre and Vladimir burst into a diabolical laughter of victory. The world was theirs. They had overthrown Eileen Lu, they had murdered
Eva Moreno, and their lackey Damien Vanderbilt was now the US president.

AMID ALL OF THESE MISHAPS, a beautiful 9-year old girl who lived
somewhere faraway, a lovely girl by the name of Sabina Hines had been awaken
of her prophecy. Pierre and Vladimir were unaware of the existence of Sabina
Hines, who was to be the only one who could save the world from their villainy.

To be continued in The Banker and the Empath.

*For more books in the same fictional universe, you can follow the travels of the
Chosen One, Sabina Hines, in* **Sabina Saves the Future,** *or you can follow Martin Orchard's world tour of villainy in* **The Fall of Martin Orchard.**

Please review:

If you got this far, please review my book. I don't care if it's a negative review if it points out why the book is bad and what can be improved. Of course, you might not score many brownie points from giving me one-star reviews, but on the other hand, what do you need brownie points for?

Don't miss out!

Visit the website below and you can sign up to receive emails whenever Martin Lundqvist publishes a new book. There's no charge and no obligation.

https://books2read.com/r/B-A-QIOG-ZINIB

BOOKS 2 READ

Connecting independent readers to independent writers.

Did you love *The Banker and the Eagle: The End of Democracy*? Then you should read *The Banker and The Dragon*[1] by Martin Lundqvist!

When a new virus emerges, one man is set to change the future.

The Australian agent Jared Pond is sent to investigate the rumours of a new Chinese bioweapon, the Hei Bai virus. During his assignment, Jared meets and falls in love with the Chinese civil rights activist Eileen Lu, the enemy of the CPOC. Together, Jared and Eileen try to uncover the dark secrets of the villainous dictator Chairman Jing Xi and his assistant Tzi Cheng. But who is Pierre Beaumont, and what is the connection between the spread of the virus and the World Bank's CEO?

Read more at martinlundqvist.com.

---

1. https://books2read.com/u/bOo8dE

2. https://books2read.com/u/bOo8dE

Also by Martin Lundqvist

Divine Space Gods
Divine Space Gods: Abraham's Follies
Divine Space Gods II: Revolution for Dummies
Divine Space Gods III: Rangda's Shenanigans

Sabina Saves the Future
Sabina's Pursuit of The Holy Grail
Sabina's Quest to Open the Portal in the Sun Pyramid
Sabina's Expedition to Stop the Apocalypse

The Banker Trilogy
The Banker and the Eagle: The End of Democracy

The Divine Zetan Trilogy
The Divine Dissimulation
The Divine Sedition
The Divine Finalisation

Standalone